OLYMPIC FATES SAGA

The Duke of Ithaca

ORIGINS DUOLOGY BOOK ONE

J.D. BRUBAKER

The Duke of Ithaca

By J. D. Brubaker

ISBN: 979-8-9882196-4-4 (e-book)

ISBN: 979-8-9882196-3-7 (Paperback)

Library of Congress Control Number: 2024906344

This book is a work of fiction. Any references to historical events, real people, or real places are used fictitiously. Other names, characters, places and events are products of the author's imagination, and any resemblances to actual events or places or persons, living or dead, is entirely coincidental.

Front cover image and book design by Angelee Van Allman.

Printed by J.D. Brubaker Books

First edition printed 2024.

jdbrubaker807@gmail.com

www.writingasajourney.com

Facebook: https://www.facebook.com/rjddanvers/

Instagram: @j.d._brubaker

Contents

Acknowledgements   1

Map of Ancient Greece   5

Map of Ancient Greece and the Aegean Sea   6

Map of the Isle of Ithaca   7

1. A Most Important Meeting   9

2. No Small Thing   15

3. Filled With Lightning   21

4. Rather Grave Business   27

5. Beloved Lady Penelope   37

6. Profound and Unhidden Desire   43

7. Flutters   55

8. Given Proper Warning   61

9. For My Daughter's Sake   67

10.	Chapter 10: Abigail's Greatest Desire	77
11.	Towards Her Future	83
12.	He Would Worship This Woman	89
13.	Welcome Home	99
14.	Yearning	107
15.	Someone of No Great Importance	117
16.	The Viscount	127
17.	Settled Back at Foxcliff Manor	137
18.	Who She Was Born to Be	145
19.	The Gods Give and the Gods Take Away	153
20.	A Royal Letter	161
21.	Reflections and Observations	169
22.	To the Mainland	179
23.	Royal Contention	191
24.	A Duke and The King	201
25.	A Duchess and The Queen	209
26.	A King's Thoughts	215
27.	A Queen's Hope	221
28.	Nearing a State of Panic	229
29.	How Close	237
30.	Slow and Steady	245
	Key List of Characters and Who They Really Are:	255

Acknowledgements

There are several people to whom I need to say an enormous thank you. Without them all, this book would never have been written.

First, I have to acknowledge the authors of the source material of these stories: Homer, Ovid, Euripides, Virgil, Hesiod, Aeschylus, Sophocles, Apuleius, and other writers of the Greek Myths.

I also must acknowledge the genius Jane Austen for writing the novels Pride and Prejudice, Mansfield Park, Persuasion, Emma, Sense and Sensibility, and Northanger Abbey; these works have been among my favorites since I was a teenager, and they gave me a profound love for the Regency period.

Second, thank you to Elaine Anderson and James Hanks for talking with me about these books, and helping me brainstorm ideas for how to take some of the more complicated aspects of the Greek myths, and adapt them to a Regency period. I was severely stumped at several points, and your perspectives allowed me to move forward with ideas and inspirations. So, thank you.

Third, as always, I simply must thank my incredible cover designer and formatter, Angelee van Allman. Seriously, your work is absolute art, and I am beyond privileged to have you for my designer. Somehow, you always take my works and design these stunning covers that fit not only the genre in which I'm writing, but also capture the essence of the books themselves. I am convinced that you have magic. Thank you so much for letting me use your talents!

Fourth, I want to say a huge thank you to Jeff McAlpine and Carol Burnell, literature professors at Clackamas Community College, where I obtained my A.S. in English. Jeff McAlpine taught Ancient World Literature, my first introduction to The Iliad and the story of Medea, and Carol Burnell taught a summer literary survey course of Ancient Greek and Roman Mythology. Without your classes, your passion for these texts, and the assignments we were given, I would not have fallen in love with these stories. Thank you for your dedication to education, and your passion for student's success.

Fifth, thank you to my beta readers: Madi Quinn, Paul Steffan, Nick Lancaster, and Susie Staplehurst. I appreciate the time, energy, and effort you put into reading this manuscript, and providing feedback. Susie, you went above and beyond and also helped me with the editing of this book, and for that I want to give you a second thank you. I appreciated every single edit you made.

Thank you as well to all of my ARC Readers! There are too many of you to name, but I cannot express enough how much you mean to me. Your time, your efforts, your enthusiasm, fill me with joy, with excitement, and with an overwhelming need to continue to write and release books for you to enjoy. So many of you are my ideal readers, and I will forever be thankful that I was able to find you.

Lastly, thank you to you, my readers, for your endless support, patience, and encouragement. There were many moments as I wrote this book where I wondered if it would ever be completed, and the one thing which kept me pushing through was the desire to give all of you an amazing, sexy, interesting book that retells some of literature's best ancient texts. Those of you on TikTok, on Facebook, on Instagram and Threads, and on Lemon8 are honestly the best readers and supporters a writer could ask for.

I hope you enjoy this book!

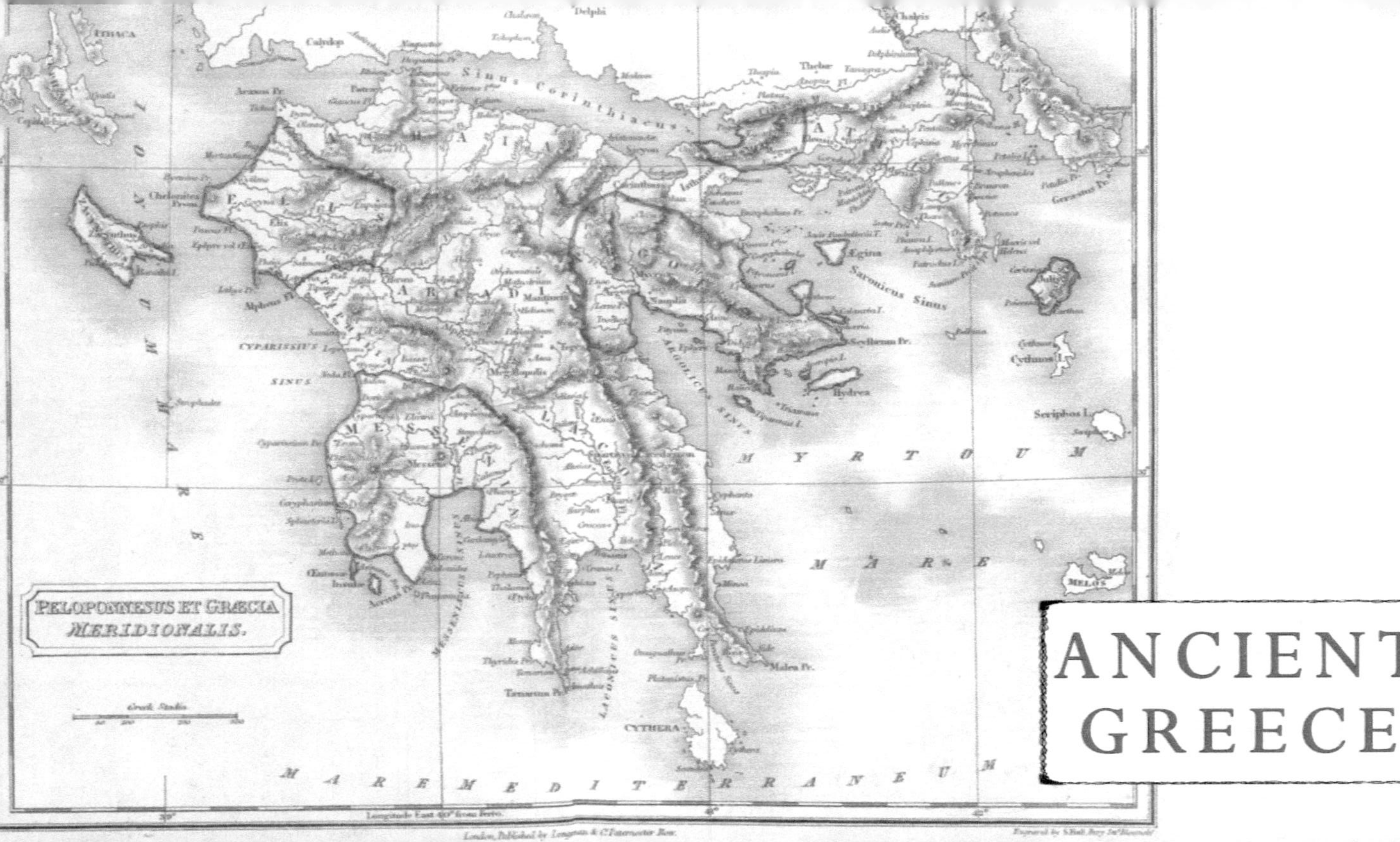

ANCIENT GREECE
PELOPONNESUS ET GRÆCIA MERIDIONALIS.
Greek Stadia
Sinus Corinthiacus
ACHAIA
ELIS
ARCADIA
MESSENIA
LACONIA
ARGOLICUS SINUS
Saronicus Sinus
CYPARISSIUS SINUS
MESSENIACUS SINUS
LACONICUS SINUS
MARE MYRTOUM
MARE MEDITERRANEUM
Delphi
Chalcis
Corinthus
Ægina
Hydrea
Messene
Lacedæmon
Sparta
Malea Pr.
Tænarum Pr.
CYTHERA
Seriphos I.
Cythnus I.
MELOS
ITHACA
Zacynthus
Longitude East 40° from Ferro.
London, Published by Longman & Co. Paternoster Row.
Engraved by S. Hall, Bury S.t Bloomsb.y

ANCIENT GREECE

AND

AEGEAN SEA

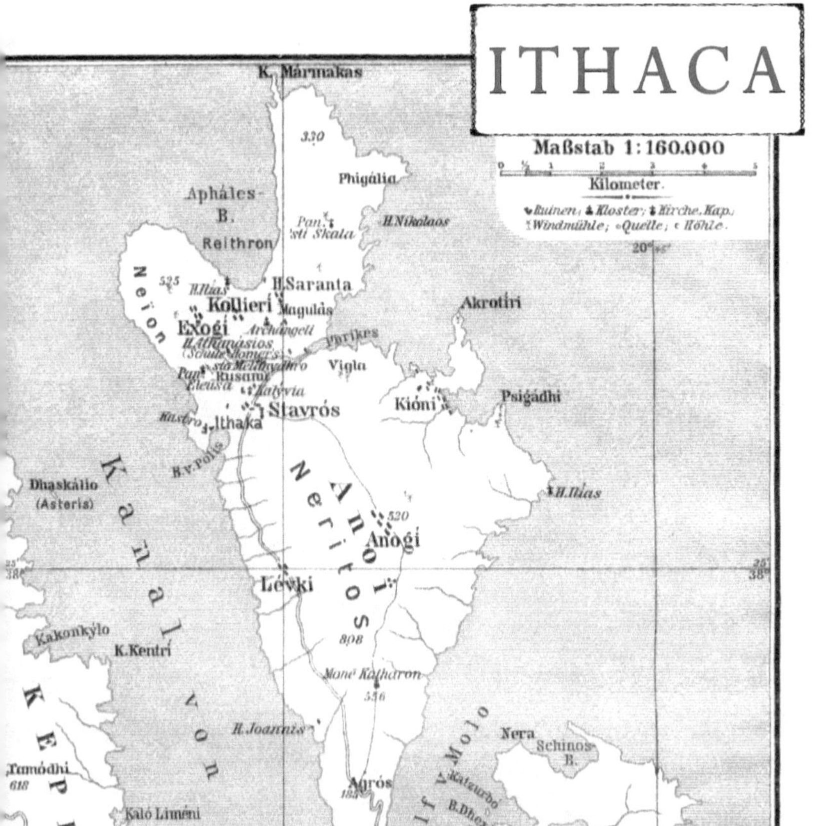

ITHACA
Maßstab 1:160.000
Kilometer.
Ruinen; Kloster; Kirche, Kap.;
Windmühle; Quelle; Höhle
K. Mármakas
330
Phigália
Apháles-
B.
Reithron
Pan. sti Skala
H. Nikólaos
Akrotíri
Neïon
525
H. Ilias
H. Saranta
Kollíeri
Magulás
Exogi
Archángeli
H. Athanásios
(Schule Homer's)
Harikes
sto Melthyathro
Vigla
Pan. Kusanu
Eleusa
Latyvia
Kióni
Psigádhi
Kastro
Ithaka
Stavrós
B. v. Polis
Dhaskálio
(Asteris)
H. Ilias
Ano i
Nerítos
520
Anógi
Lévki
Kakonkýlo
K. Kentri
808
Mone Katharon
556
H. Joánnis
Nera
Schinos
B.
Tamódhi
618
Agrós
184
Golf v. Molo
Katzurbo
B. Dhexia
B. v.
Wathy
K.
Sarakiniko
Kaló Liméni
H. Spiridhon
Kanelata
H.
Sophia
Höhle
Wathy
(Ithake)
Aëtós
300
430
Komitata
Alalkomenai
H. Georgios
671
Perachorio
Pissaëto
Merovigli
Gaïanna
Stephani
Ligiá
Neochori
B. v.
Perapégadhi
Pan. sto Antolikó
Taxiárchis
sto Vuni
Perapégadhi
Arethusa
Korax
H. Joánnes
sto Elleniko
Marathiá
280
Agriósyko
H.
Joannis
H. Evphimia
20°40'
Ostl. L. v. Greenw.
B. M. Andreas
Geograph. Anstalt v. Wagner & Debes, Leipzig.

CHAPTER ONE

A Most Important Meeting

March, 13th Century B.C.E.
Foxcliff Manor,
Perachori, Ithaca
Greece

The early spring morning was damp. Odysseus Halstead, Duke of Ithaca, loved walking the grounds of his estate every morning before the rest of the house was awake. He didn't know if it was the silence, the tranquility, or just the freedom to connect with the land that he called his own; whatever it was, morning walks in the pre-dawn twilight filled him with a sense that everything was right with the world. He relished those moments because he knew all too well that everything was not right, and yet he felt it could be if he willed it hard enough.

Maybe he couldn't make everything right for the world, but he could make everything right for *his* world. And he intended to do just that. His mind wandered to the ball he had held only a few nights before. Odysseus wasn't much of one for balls and parties, but he saw how much the people of Ithaca enjoyed them, and so he obliged them as frequently as he could stand.

The last ball had been held for no other reason than to give the people within his dukedom a little fun. The ongoing war between Greece and Troy was a point of much turmoil for his people as more and more of their young men were shipped off to battle, and Odysseus felt it was his solemn duty to give them as much comfort as he could. It pleased him to do so, and also provided him the opportunity to dance with the woman he intended to marry.

Miss Penelope Auckland was the only child and heiress of Earl Icarius Auckland, one of the most respectable men in Ithaca. Odysseus had met Penelope some months before and, within the short period that had passed since then, he had come to feel a passionate desire to make her his wife. Indeed, he could do so simply by commanding it, such was his right as a duke.

But that was beneath him, he knew, and disrespectful to not only her station, but also her person. Odysseus didn't want to be accepted by default. He wanted her to choose him as much as he was choosing her, even if that meant she ultimately rejected his suit. For was not that the very definition of love and respect? The freedom to choose?

He rounded the corner of his home, the large estate called Foxcliff Manor, and made his way towards the front entrance. He had left the door open and grinned when he saw his dog, Simon, waiting for him. Simon saw him coming and began to wag his tail. Odysseus motioned for him to follow and they made their way inside. His valet would come by his room soon to dress him, and then Odysseus would break his fast. Then, if he could muster the courage, he would head to Lord Auckland's land to ask his permission to marry his daughter. If he was granted that permission, and Odysseus could think of no reason why he wouldn't be, then he would go and make his suit to Penelope herself.

His heart thundered in his chest at the very thought. It wasn't that he was deeply in love with Penelope. Not yet, at least. They had only known each other for a few months. But he felt keenly that she was the woman he wanted to build a life with, and he believed that love and romance would come quickly if given the chance. Her vivacity, her playful demeanor, and her sharp cleverness were becoming for a potential duchess, as well as a potential life partner. He felt himself falling in love with her, and had for over a month now, but it was the ball four nights passed that confirmed it.

He had watched her dance with several other men before summoning the courage to ask her himself. She had grinned up at him with those bright blue eyes that so fully captivated his attention and said, "I would be honored, Duke Halstead. Indeed, I've been wondering if you were ever going to ask me at all."

He had offered her his hand and escorted her onto the dance floor. "Really? What made you think I would?"

"Any man who stares at a woman from across the room for nearly two full hours together is either plotting her murder, or planning to ask her to dance."

He had grinned widely, barely holding in his laughter. "Is that so?"

She nodded. "It is so, yes. And since I could think of no reason why you should want to witness my demise, I assumed you were planning to solicit my hand for a dance."

"And there could be no other alternative explanations, then?"

She shook her head, her dark curls bouncing against her neck as she did so. "None whatsoever."

Odysseus had been too shocked to say much at the time. The look in her eyes and the nonchalant tone of her voice told him she was joking, and indeed the wink she offered in the next moment confirmed it. Odysseus had wanted to tease her back, to show that he was just as capable of playfulness as she, but his mind had been blank, utterly devoid of anything witty or clever, and he had merely smiled at her.

They danced together for several dances in succession. He didn't recall how many exactly. He only knew that they stopped when another gentleman stepped forward and asked for the chance to dance with her. It was bad form to take up all of a woman's time at a ball, and so he graciously bowed and removed himself from the dance floor. He had gone to one of the tables near the side of the room and grabbed a glass of wine, and then turned and pretended to watch everyone else dance, though in truth, his eyes had been ever on Penelope Auckland.

He had then been approached by Emerson Arrow, the owner of nearly every hot house in Ithaca where people could purchase bouquets of flowers as well as fruits and vegetables. His roses were especially sought after, and was why he always wore a rose shaped pendant on his coat. Mr. Arrow had smiled at Odysseus and then cast a glance towards Penelope as she danced with another gentleman.

"She is a beauty, is she not, Your Grace?" he had asked.

Odysseus nodded. "Indeed, she is."

"I do believe people are rather excited at your choosing to dance so long with Lady Penelope," said Mr. Arrow.

"Oh?" he asked, turning to face the man.

He nodded. "Yes. I have heard several people whisper about how fine you looked together." He gave Odysseus a knowing look and a wink. "I think they might suspect a forthcoming engagement, although who can really say for sure." He placed his hand on Odysseus' shoulder. "If you do choose her, Your Grace, I am sure you will be most happy."

That conversation had lived in his mind for days now, and in truth, Odysseus felt as though it had been the precise moment when he'd determined within himself that yes, he would propose to Penelope Auckland.

Odysseus climbed the stairs to his bedchamber and threw himself onto the bed. He had admired several women throughout his life, and had even fancied himself in love once before, but no one had ever captured him the way Penelope did. Even when he had nearly proposed to a young woman three years prior, his feelings for her were nothing compared to what he felt for Penelope. It was not merely desire, although he could not deny the flutters in his belly or the lust that grew deeper inside of him at the very thought of her. Those bright blue eyes that sparkled with a love for life and living; the raven-black curls that accentuated her fair features so well; the figure that practically drove him wild with passion. She was a beautiful woman, there was no denying that. And he did, indeed, desire her physically. There was no denying that, either.

But he also felt a profound respect and admiration that separated her above all other women. Her mind was quick, and her knowledge stretched far beyond what most women of her rank were expected to know. He had inquired into her education and discovered that she had been given the best governess and the best tutors. She had studied not only those subjects befitting a young woman of noble birth, but also mathematics, geography, science, and even the basics of agriculture. She could dance, sew, sing, played both the piano and the harp, and yet she could also shoot and hunt.

To him, Penelope Auckland was perfection. There was no other woman like her in all of his extensive acquaintance, and he would not let another day pass without pressing his suit to her. If she rejected him, or if her father did not grant his permission, he would walk away graciously. He would treat her no differently than he did now, and he would wish her all the happiness in the world. He would mean it, too. But he could not deny that he would be gravely disappointed. Odysseus truly did not think he would ever find another woman who made him feel the way she did.

But he would not know if his fate and hers would ever overlap, or if they would remain individual threads, sometimes meeting, but never walking together, until he proposed. He rang for his valet and began to prepare for what would likely be one of the most important meetings of his life.

CHAPTER TWO
No Small Thing

Wovenspell Abbey

Perachori, Ithaca

Greece

Odysseus stood at the window and stared out at the garden near the side of Lord Icarius Auckland's house. He had been shown into the drawing room when he arrived, and the butler said he would inform Lord Auckland of his arrival. Since then, some fifteen minutes had passed, and Odysseus was beginning to think Lord Auckland might not come and see him after all. He had tried to distract himself in a number of ways. None had worked. So now he contented himself with staring out at the garden, his mind floating always back to Penelope and the growing fear that her father would not give his permission.

"Ah, Lord Halstead," came a voice from behind him that Odysseus knew to be Lord Auckland.

Odysseus turned and smiled at the man. They bowed to one another and then shook hands.

"I am terribly sorry to have kept you waiting," Lord Auckland said, motioning for Odysseus to sit. "I was in the middle of writing a letter to my sister in Athens and nearly forgot you had arrived."

Odysseus smiled and shook his head. "No apologies are necessary, I assure you. I was merely admiring the garden out that window. It is very well kept."

Lord Auckland nodded. "That is all my daughter's work. She loves tending the garden and has done so since she was a child. Indeed, I think if I had let her run around barefoot, she'd still be doing so today."

Both men laughed. Odysseus liked the idea of Penelope Auckland running through the grass, the dirt, and the mud; an earl's daughter, heiress to the Auckland estate of Wovenspell Abbey, not afraid of getting herself dirty. It was a pleasant thought, indeed.

"So, to what do I owe the honor of your visit?" Lord Auckland asked, although Odysseus could tell by the look on the man's face that the question was really just a formality. He knew precisely what had brought Odysseus, Duke of Ithaca, to his home.

"I have come here today, sir, to ask your permission to propose to your daughter," Odysseus said, cutting straight to the point. "I think you must have observed an attachment forming between us of late, and I have come to want nothing more than to have Penelope by my side, as my wife."

It was a simple statement that Odysseus hoped would please Lord Auckland. The Earl, Odysseus knew, was not a man of many words and did not enjoy fancy speeches. By being precise and direct, he hoped Lord Auckland would see the seriousness of his intentions and give his consent. But as Odysseus watched the man, he could see instantly that this was not going to be an easy conversation.

"Do you know how many men have asked for my permission to marry my daughter?" Lord Auckland asked, the friendliness leaving his eyes. He did not wait for Odysseus to reply. "Four," he said with emphasis. "Four men before you have made a similar suit for my daughter's hand in marriage, and I gave none of them my permission. Do you know why?"

Odysseus felt his heart begin to race. He had not been so foolish as to believe he was the first or only suitor attempting to win Penelope's affections, but he had not considered that perhaps other offers of marriage had already been made to her. Indeed, he knew of no other men who had asked for her hand, and to now hear that there had been four such men set him on edge.

"I assume you did not give your consent because you knew they would not be good matches for Lady Penelope," Odysseus replied, trying hard to hide the panic in his voice.

Lord Auckland nodded slowly. "Partly. But my opinion of them is less important than her own. The four who sought her hand were four men for whom she had explicitly expressed disdain. However pleasant she had been in public when decorum required it of her, she always made sure I knew her true feelings. Especially that Viscount Antinous Capshaw. He was the first to seek her hand and he did not take my refusal kindly."

Odysseus was particularly surprised now. He knew for a fact that Antinous Capshaw had been paying court to another young woman in Ithaca. Indeed, he had made it abundantly clear what his intentions were towards Miss Abigail Webb, and now had asked permission to marry a completely different woman? Odysseus made note of it. He would have to pay a visit to Viscont Capshaw.

"Perhaps I can clarify my intentions in coming to see you, Lord Auckland?" Odysseus asked and, when Lord Auckland did not refuse, he continued. "I am not here simply because I believe your daughter to be a desirable catch. I am here offering her my hand in marriage because I admire her. I respect her and your family. And I believe that I can make her happy, which is the bare minimum that she deserves."

"And certainly her dowry of £30,000 *and* inheritance of this estate upon my death would make you incredibly happy as well," Lord Auckland said, his gaze staring ever into Odysseus' eyes. "You cannot really imagine me ignorant of how often such information is spread around the communities of bachelors, can you?"

Odysseus' palms began to sweat. He had thought his explanation sufficient in communicating that his intentions had very little to do with money, and now wondered if, perhaps, he had completely miscalculated this meeting.

"No, sir. I am aware that these details are common knowledge among those groups of men looking to find a wife. And I did not mean to imply that I am indifferent to your daughter's rank and fortune. I merely wanted to convey that her dowry and inheritance play only a little role in my desire to make your daughter my wife. Indeed, above the money, I count her intelligence, her wit, her knowledge of how to run an estate, and her compassion for others among the highest qualities she possesses."

Lord Auckland nodded slowly. "The others said much the same thing. Well, except for Lord Capshaw who admitted openly that he was really only interested in her inheritance." He leaned forward and placed his elbows on his knees. "Answer me this: what kind of husband would you be?"

Odysseus furrowed his eyebrows. "Kind of husband, sir?"

He nodded. "Yes. What kind of husband would you be? Attentive? Caring? Ambivalent? Cold? Absent?"

Odysseus saw his chance. "I would be the best husband I could be. Not merely in the typical duties expected of one such as myself, but also in the assurance of her day-to-day wellbeing." He cleared his throat. "At the risk of sounding desperate, sir, I do not hesitate to tell you that I believe I am falling in love with Penelope. And my hope, my goal for every single waking moment with her would be to do my utmost to provide her with whatever she wants or needs to be happy." He grinned. "I would not treat her as an object or a trophy, for I do not view her as such. She is my equal – nay, she is my superior, for no other woman on earth has ever made me want to be a better man than I am. If given the chance, sir, I would live each day to better myself so that, hopefully, by the time I am old and dying, I will be able to say that I did, eventually, come to deserve her love and devotion."

Lord Auckland was smiling brightly by the time Odysseus was done, though he did not say anything for nearly five minutes.

"I should tell you, your lordship, that I had decided to give you my permission before I even walked into this room," he said at last.

Odysseus raised his eyebrows. "You had?"

He nodded. "Penelope has spoken of you to me several times and it has been some weeks now that I have suspected her to be growing attached to you."

Odysseus smiled widely, caring not that he likely looked like a silly school boy. Knowing that Penelope had talked positively of him to her father at all gave him immense hope for her acceptance of his proposal. Hearing that she had spoken of him fondly enough that her father could see the tenderness in her feelings, was more than he could have hoped for.

"Indeed, Lord Halstead, it has been a great balm to my old heart to see her admire someone enough to love them. Or to, at least, be open to that love. Therefore, I cannot but grant you my blessing and leave you to make your suit to her." He stood to his feet and held out his hand for Odysseus to shake. "And I do so gladly."

Odysseus stood, took the man's hand, and shook it.

"Penelope is in the back garden," Lord Auckland said.

"Thank you, Lord Auckland," he said, and then quickly moved away, his heart thundering in his chest.

He had obtained her father's permission, and that had been no small thing. But would he get hers? That he did not know for sure. He felt a great deal of hope and some confidence, given Lord Auckland's account of Penelope's feelings for him, but he dared not enter the garden believing her acceptance to be guaranteed. He would celebrate only when she had accepted his hand, and not a moment sooner.

CHAPTER THREE
Filled With Lightning

It was early spring, barely a month since winter had faded away, and the morning had shifted from cold and damp to warm and dry. The sun shone brightly in the clear blue sky and, for the first time since winter, the flowers in the garden had begun to bloom. Twenty-two year old Penelope Auckland smiled down at them as they opened towards the warming sunshine, as though eager to absorb its rays.

It wasn't only the flowers that had come alive in the unexpected sunshine. Honey bees buzzed around her, landing on flowers to drink their nectar. Penelope talked to them as they flew around her, seemingly uninterested in the woman as they went about their hive's business.

"I'm sure your queen will be pleased with all of your work," she said, resisting the urge to reach out and try to get some of them into the palm of her hand. The bees were used to her presence and often did land on her to rest and bathe themselves. It was one of her favorite things, but being one of the first truly calm and sunny days of the season, she knew this sojourn out of their hive was vitally important. So she let them be as they flew from bulb to bulb, blossom to blossom, drinking nectar and spreading pollen.

Penelope took great pleasure in spending time in her garden. She often returned indoors covered in dirt and mud, much to the horror of her maids, but it wasn't something she ever intended to give up. If and when she managed her own home, she would make a garden for herself, a haven where she could read or even just sit and listen to the wind as it blew by. And always, she would be there to tend it.

The sound of approaching footsteps interrupted her reverie. She turned her head to see who was coming up the stone walkway and nearly gasped as Lord Odysseus Halstead, the Duke of Ithaca, walked towards her. She looked back to the flowers as she attempted to compose herself, but inwardly, her heart raced. Had he come to merely pay his respects after a successful ball some days before? Or was he here on more personal business? She hoped for the latter, but was pleased that he had come to see her at all.

She rose to her feet and faced him, suddenly very conscious of the dirt on her apron. "Lord Halstead," she said with a curtsey, "I am pleased to see you. To what do I owe this surprise?"

Penelope noticed that he seemed quite nervous. He could hardly meet her gaze for more than a few seconds together before looking away and blushing. She forced herself not to laugh or tease him, as she didn't think either one would lessen his anxiety.

"I trust you are well, Lady Penelope?" he said at last, forcing himself to meet her gaze and not look away.

She smiled. "I am doing very well, your lordship. A day that begins in my garden is always a good day, indeed. And made even better when the Duke of Ithaca comes to call." She smiled sweetly, only daring to be so bold because she wanted him to know how glad she was to see him.

He grinned. "I suppose I should get to the point, should I not?"

She cocked her head to the side. "You mean you didn't come all the way here simply to keep me company?"

His grin widened. "Well, Lady Penelope, that's actually what I wanted to talk with you about. The truth is," he said, taking a step forward, "I wish to always keep your company. I never want to be without you by my side."

She could see he was so nervous, he was practically shaking, and her own nerves began to intensify as she listened to his speech. It was one thing to suspect why he'd come; it was another thing entirely to hear his professions made so directly.

"I wish I were better at expressing myself, but I hope that I can impress upon you the fervency of my growing love and devotion. I hope, indeed, Lady Penelope that there is no misunderstanding here, and that you have seen what my feelings are and have been of late. I especially hope that you will take me in earnest when I ask if you would consent to be my wife."

Penelope wanted to laugh and cry simultaneously. She was happier than she could ever have imagined she would be. Not merely because Odysseus had actually proposed, but also that his feelings were sincere and apparent. Her biggest fear hadn't been that he wouldn't propose; she had been almost certain he would eventually, given the special attention he had paid to her over the last few months. What she hadn't been able to determine was whether or not his attentions had been fostered out of real love and admiration, or duty. He was the only remaining living member of his family. He had a duty to his ancestors and to the people who depended on him for employment, like his tenants and servants. He needed an heir. Penelope had been afraid that he would ask her to marry him to satisfy his duties as a duke and owner of an estate. And while she probably would have accepted him regardless, it made her heart soar to think that he held feelings for her that went beyond duty.

She smiled up at him. "You are quite nervous, my lord. I hope that my father did not make things too difficult for you."

He grinned and shook his head. "No less than was his right."

Penelope laughed then, heartily pleased at the idea of her father, an Earl of Ithaca, setting the Duke of Ithaca on his guard and unnerving him to this extent. "I am his only child," she said, "and he is rather protective of me."

Odysseus nodded. "He loves you greatly. I do not fault him for a moment." His amused grin turned to one of tenderness. "I do, however, hope that my shattered nerves and poorly expressed feelings are sufficient to show you the sincerity of my intentions."

Penelope took a step towards him. "They are, indeed," she said, feeling as though she couldn't continue to leave him in suspense. "I confess, your lordship, that this is a meeting I have hoped for for some time. Your kindness, your generosity, and your gentleness have appealed to me over the last few months, and it has been some weeks now that I have sincerely wished for you to make your suit."

Odysseus' eyes brightened. "Then...you are accepting my offer of marriage?"

She nodded. "I am. With my whole heart and soul."

His arms were around her waist the next moment, holding her to him in a tight embrace. His body shook with laughter as he held her close and she, in turn, wrapped her arms around his neck. She closed her eyes, feeling her heart expand with happiness until she thought it would burst. It was some moments before he broke the embrace and stepped back to look down into her face.

"Would it be too forward of me to ask permission to kiss you?"

She laughed. "Gods above, I wish you would," she said.

He leaned in quickly at first and then slowed himself, as though wanting to savor the moment. Penelope's heart rushed with emotions and flutters filled her belly. She had never been kissed before. She was not so naive as to believe it would be his first kiss too, but that did not matter to her. As his lips pressed against hers gently, she felt as though her entire body was filled with lightning. One press against her lips led to two, two led to three, and in the next moment they were holding each other again, only much more intimately. By the time they ended the embrace and returned to the house to confirm the engagement with her father, Penelope could think only one thing: that she could not wait until the wedding night.

CHAPTER FOUR

Rather Grave Business

Odysseus spent the remainder of the morning and early afternoon with Penelope and her father. Lord Auckland beamed with pride at the announcement. It was clear that seeing his daughter so happy was a great relief to him. The man was old, after all. It was well known that he and his late wife had tried for years to produce an heir, and failed. When Penelope's mother did finally fall pregnant, she was considerably older than was usual and her pregnancy had caused many complications. She had died in childbirth, leaving Icarius to care for baby Penelope alone. By then, he was well into his fifties. Now, some twenty years later, his health was failing rapidly and it was believed he would not live for more than a few years. It was good, Odysseus thought, that the man should welcome the end of his life knowing that his daughter, his only child, would be taken care of and cherished.

The three of them enjoyed each other's company over luncheon, and Lord Auckland frequently smiled through eyes glistening with tears as he watched Penelope and her beloved. He was proud, indeed. And, as he told Odysseus, he would have been lying if he said he wasn't excited to see his girl marrying a duke, especially one graced with the friendship and benevolence of Menelaus, King of Greece. It was an eligible match, to be sure. And when the time came for him to leave, Odysseus promised that he would return on the morrow to continue the newfound intimacy between their houses.

He also intended to develop greater intimacy between himself and his betrothed. Because the two were now officially engaged, he and Penelope were allowed a deeper level of intimacy and privacy, making it much easier for them to get to know each other better. It was preferable to him that they be as close as they could when they wed, for he did not want there to be any awkwardness or tension. Or, at least, none that would be considered negative. This was more for her sake than his own, for he was a man of the world. His innocence and naivety had been gone for some years, but he did not expect that even a young woman of Penelope's education would understand everything about the relationship between a husband and wife. He did not want her to be apprehensive in any way. Not if he could help it.

Before he climbed into his carriage, he quietly instructed his valet not to return to Foxcliff, but to instead head towards Laketon Place, the home of Viscount Antinous Capshaw. They had much to discuss now that he knew of Capshaw's less than honorable behaviors towards both Penelope and the other woman he had been courting. Usually, Odysseus tried to keep out of the goings on of the other lords. It was within his right, due to his rank and station, to take a keener interest in their actions, but he found such controlling ways to be beneath him as well as insulting to those whom he, mostly, considered friends.

Viscount Capshaw was one of the only exceptions.

He was widely known to be a rake, which was not uncommon among the bachelors of nobility, and that on its own was not enough to deter Odysseus' respect. But it was the ways in which Antinous talked of women that made Odysseus' skin crawl. He firmly believed the man was a fiend who cared about nothing but his own personal advantage. That, too, was not so uncommon, but even those men who primarily or solely married for money and station at least carried some respect for the women they courted. Antinous acted like a petulant school boy and showed no respect for anyone beyond himself.

Odysseus arrived at the Viscount's home a few moments later and was ushered into one of the small drawing rooms near the front of the large house. Antinous was the youngest son of his family and had originally been intended for the Navy. But when his father and three older brothers died suddenly in a drunken brawl in Athens, Antinous had inherited everything. He had been merely nineteen at that time and, even now at the young age of twenty-three, was less than what a Viscount should be in his conduct and attitudes.

"Lord Halstead," the young man exclaimed when he came into the drawing room. He smiled, bowed to Odysseus, and then held out his hand. "I am delighted to see you. What brings you here on this fine day?"

Odysseus shook his hand and sat on one of the sofas. "To be honest, Capshaw, I'm here on some rather grave business."

Antinous raised his eyebrows and nodded slowly. "I see. Well, if I can be of any assistance, I shall do my best to aid you."

Odysseus grinned halfheartedly. Antinous was known to be agreeable to those when it suited his needs and wants. Indeed, the young man had never liked Odysseus and had said as much to some of the other nobles in Ithaca when he thought Odysseus was not within earshot. Antinous did not know Odysseus had heard every word spoken, else he might not have been so friendly with the duke this morning. Odysseus wasn't about to let his cheerful, engaging manner deter him from his task.

"I wanted to let you know that I am, as of this morning, engaged to be married," Odysseus said, not wanting to begin the conversation by accusing Antinous of anything untoward.

Antinous grinned, his fair features giving him the look of a man much younger than he was. "Indeed? I am glad to hear it. I must confess, it has been some time that the rest of us have wondered whether or not you would ever take a wife."

"Well, I have been very careful in my choice of future partner, and I can say confidently that the waiting was worth it."

"And who, may I ask, is the lucky woman?"

"Miss Penelope Auckland," Odysseus said, more eager to see Antinous' reaction than he probably should have been.

Antinous did not respond and his expression did not change much. It was clear the man was fighting an influx of emotions and did not want to offend the duke sitting before him. Odysseus felt a twinge of pleasure, knowing that he had snuffed out whatever hopes Antinous had still held for potentially obtaining Penelope as his wife in the future. If he held such hopes.

"And to speak the truth, Lord Capshaw, I am a bit bewildered by a report I was given this morning when I spoke with Lord Auckland about my desire to marry his daughter. He told me that you were one of the previous suitors who had come to ask his permission for her hand." Odysseus paused and let his words penetrate Antinous' mind before continuing. "And I found that incredibly odd considering the many attentions you have been paying to Miss Webb of late. I was hoping you could clear this up for me." Antinous opened his mouth to speak, but Odysseus interrupted him. "Because I certainly would not like to believe that one of the nobles under my influence would openly pay court to one young woman while secretly making designs on another. Such behavior would be unbecoming and, well," he shrugged, "grounds for me to take action."

Darkness fell over Antinous' features. All friendliness and ease of manner was gone, replaced by what seemed to be intense anger and offense. Odysseus knew the rest of this conversation would not go well, but he would not back down. This was his duty and Antinous Capshaw needed to be set right.

"Action? What action, my lord?" he asked, his voice rigid and no longer friendly, as it had been before.

"Well, when an heir inherits their father's land and title, there are vows he must take regarding duty and honor and decency. As noblemen, much is expected of us. We set the standard for everyone else, and if a noble within my influence were to behave so wretchedly as to elevate one young woman's hope of marriage when he never intended to marry that woman in the first place, and then, indeed, went to press his marital suit to another young woman instead, I would be faced with a serious dilemma. One I think I could only resolve by stripping that man of his land and title."

Antinous' pale cheeks flared with rage. "I hope, Lord Halstead, that you are not implying that these have been my actions or that such recourse would be your response. I do not take kindly to threats."

"And I do not take kindly to people mistreating those I have been given the responsibility to govern. Miss Webb is a respectable woman from a respectable family. It is common knowledge that you have paid her special attention for the last several months."

"I have made Miss Webb no promises –" he started, but Odysseus interrupted him.

"It is such common knowledge, in fact, that many have spoken of your engagement as a settled thing."

Antinous shook his head and attempted to laugh nonchalantly. "People gossip, my lord. I cannot help that."

"Perhaps it is idle gossip, but it did not come from nothing. Do you deny spending multiple evenings at the Webb residence in the last few months?"

"No, but –"

"And were these visits initiated by yourself, or were you there as her father's guest?"

Antinous's cheeks turned red as he tried to keep his temper in check. "I initiated them, however –"

"I know from your own admissions at other times that you made plans to visit Miss Webb and her family on numerous occasions, so at the very least, Lord Capshaw, you have behaved carelessly. At worst, you have behaved maliciously. Both are grounds for me to take extreme actions against you."

Antinous' anger was replaced by fear. "Please, Lord Halstead, I meant no disrespect either to Lady Penelope or to Miss Webb. I made a foolish mistake. It was, indeed, my design to press my suit to Miss Webb, but when I first became acquainted with Lady Penelope, I was struck and infatuated. I rushed to press my suit before I thought any of it through, and her father, the good man, saw through all of my words and denied my request for his consent."

"He said you told him outright that you desired her for her inheritance and her sizable dowry," Odysseus said, not believing any of Antinous' justifications and excuses.

"Again, a foolish decision. I didn't think he would believe me if I claimed to love his daughter, having known her for such a short time, and so I opted for blunt honesty instead. The truth was that I cared not for her inheritance or her dowry, but I made an absolute fool of myself regardless and he denied me."

Odysseus nodded slowly. "And what is your plan now?"

"Sir?"

"You said your original intention was to marry Miss Webb. Is that still your intention?"

The Viscount hesitated. "Well, to be honest, Your Grace –"

Odysseus stood to his feet. "I think I've heard all that I must. I confess myself disappointed beyond measure, Lord Capshaw. Neither your father nor any of your brothers would have behaved in this way. The question now becomes how I should act in light of what I've just been told."

Antinous stood to his feet, his eyes ablaze with fear. "Please, your lordship, I beg of you. Do not take my title or my lands. I will do anything you ask of me. I will remake myself. I will atone. Please."

Odysseus stared at him. He was not convinced that this appeal to his mercy was sincere, although the fear in Antinous' eyes was most convincing. Still, Odysseus did not believe the man was genuine in his promise to remake himself and atone, though he believed it his duty to give him a chance to do so.

"If you wish to remain a Viscount, you will go and ask Mr. Webb for his permission to marry his daughter." Antinous' disappointment was evident, but he nodded. "You will marry the girl and you will do right by her. She is a good young woman who has been brought up honorably and I will not see her joyful spirit dashed because of you." Again, Antinous nodded. "And if I hear so much as a general peep from anyone regarding mistreatment, infidelity, or neglect of her, I will not only strip away your lands and title, I will, in turn, give them to her and annul the marriage between you."

Antinous' eyes widened. "That would ruin me!" he shouted.

"Then I suggest you heed the seriousness of my words, Viscount Capshaw. And be grateful I do not pass this information on to the King. Do you imagine that he would be more merciful and gracious than I have been?"

Antinous lowered his gaze and shook his head, but Odysseus could practically taste his rage.

"I had better hear of your engagement soon, Viscount Capshaw. If you truly do wish to remake yourself and atone for the actions that have made this meeting necessary, then you will heed my words and do as I have instructed," Odysseus said before seeing himself out.

He sighed as he climbed back into his carriage. It wasn't that he thought Antinous would have completely jilted Miss Webb, although that certainly was a possibility. She may not have been the daughter of an Earl, but her father was a prestigious and well respected man in the community. The Webbs were one of the oldest families in Ithaca and, considering their high standing in his favor and the favor of the county, the match would still be very eligible for Antinous Capshaw.

It was, therefore, likely that he would have still made his suit eventually. Likely, but not certain. There weren't many other eligible women among the noble families, or at least none that were yet ready for something like marriage, so he would have either had to wait to secure his place in Ithacan society, or marry Miss Webb. The question was which choice he would have made if left to his own devices. Antinous had already exemplified that he was perfectly comfortable leading Miss Webb into assumptions of marriage while secretly looking for a more advantageous match. Odysseus would not let that happen a second time.

He was aware, too, that forcing Antinous to marry Miss Webb was inviting trouble. He hoped that his orders to the young Viscount would prohibit too much sadness and marital strife, but he did not bank on it. That was why he secretly intended to write to the king and urge him to confer on Mr. Webb the title of Baron. This would mean nothing to Miss Webb. If she did, indeed, marry Antinous, she would be a Viscountess. And on the chance that Antinous was not an ideal husband, she would remain a Viscountess, even if the marriage unraveled, as Odysseus had threatened.

But should Antinous ultimately decide not to press his suit to Abigail, as was still a possibility, even with Odysseus' threats, the barony settled on her father would then become her inheritance. There were many other nobles in search of a wife like her. She would not want admirers. If Antinous ultimately did not propose to her, Odysseus would have to decide how to act. When he threatened Antinous with the loss of his land and title, he had meant every word. Although strictly speaking, he did not have the authority to strip Antinous of anything. Only the king did. And while Menelaus almost always granted Odysseus' requests, it didn't necessarily follow that he would do in this case.

If Antinous realized this discrepancy in Odysseus' half-deceit, he could refuse to marry Miss Webb out of spite. If so, Odysseus intended to ensure that she would still make an excellent marriage. The barony would do just that. And it wouldn't hurt to impress upon Antinous just how much sway Odysseus had with King Menelaus. That on its own might be enough to convince Antinous to marry Miss Webb.

CHAPTER FIVE

Beloved Lady Penelope

Late March, 13th Century B.C.E.
Wovenspell Abbey,
Perachori, Ithaca
Greece

Penelope looked around the drawing room, her blue eyes wide and sparkling with excitement. The engagement between her and Odysseus had been publicly announced, and already presents were being delivered by the other noble and gentle families in Ithaca. The drawing room was so full, the servants thought they might need to start storing presents in the billiard room. Lord Auckland objected to this as one of his favorite pastimes was billiards, and so instead they settled on putting the presents in the library.

Odysseus came by most evenings to dine with his soon-to-be wife and father-in-law. The more time the three of them spent together, the happier Penelope felt. She saw a great deal of similarities between the two men, and that only made her love them both that much more. They got along very well and, to Penelope's enjoyment, found that they shared many lived experiences. Like Odysseus, Lord Auckland was also an only child who had inherited his father's estate and title at a young age. And, like Odysseus, Lord Auckland had waited many years to find a potential bride that he loved and respected before pressing his suit.

After the first week of preparations for the wedding, Penelope held a luncheon at her father's home and invited her three closest friends: Lady Persephone Darkworth, daughter of the Marquiss of Kioni; Lady Eurydice Hartman, daughter of the Baron of Anoge, and Lady Medea Wright, daughter of the King of Colchis. Persephone and Eurydice were native Ithacans, but Medea had left her home in Colchis to travel the world. She had settled in Ithaca and become close friends with Penelope almost immediately.

It was early afternoon when the four of them sat down for tea in the parlor. Penelope had instructed the cook to make sandwiches with cucumbers, thyme, and thinly sliced chicken, as well as an assortment of pastries, sliced cheeses with bread, and strawberries with cream. The ladies sat at a square table near the window. They ate, drank tea, and enjoyed each other's company as good friends do.

After their initial greetings and mundane chit-chat, Medea smiled at Penelope from across the table. "And so you are the first of our merry group to secure a husband."

"Well, she hasn't secured him yet," said Persephone with a wink at Penelope.

"Indeed, there are several weeks between now and that fateful day," added Eurydice, "and there's no telling what might happen to forego the wedding."

Penelope smiled good humoredly. "Are you speaking a bit of prophecy, Eurydice?"

The four women laughed.

"I might be. You'll only know when the wedding day comes, I suppose."

"Truly, though, Penelope," Medea said, smiling at her friend. "We are so very happy for you. We know how much you've liked him and have been hoping for this very thing to happen."

"Indeed," added Persephone, "although the gods know that the rest of us could use a bit of encouragement. It's not as though we're getting any younger."

Penelope laughed. "You're not a day older than eighteen, Persephone."

"I'm not a single day closer to marriage either," Persephone countered with a pout, "and even with my family's fortune, my dowry, and my inheritance, not a single young man has come courting."

"Perhaps you shouldn't be looking for a young man?" Eurydice said, taking a sip of her tea. "There are several eligible women you could marry, too."

"Two of them are at this very table," Medea said with a chuckle.

Persephone laughed. "I would be truly flattered to be courted by either one of you," she said, "but alas, I do not think I have the right temperament to marry a woman."

Penelope furrowed her brows curiously. "What do you mean?"

The young woman shrugged. "I don't entirely know, to be honest. But until you lot brought me into your group, I've never really got on with other women. I can't imagine I'd have any more luck with one looking for a wife."

Medea nodded. "I understand what you mean," she said. "Especially among other women of noble rank. There's a certain superficiality that makes personal connections and intimacy rather complicated."

"Are you saying it's any different with noblemen?" Penelope asked.

"No," Medea said, "but at least with them we know what they want."

"And what's that?" asked Eurydice.

"Their bits in our mouths," said Persephone.

The four of them laughed heartily and Penelope nearly spat out her tea.

"Such is what our beloved Lady Penelope here has to look forward to on her wedding night," Medea said, wagging her eyebrows playfully.

Eurydice's eyes were wide with surprise as she looked at Penelope. "Are you...really going to...use your mouth?" she asked, her voice quieting to a whisper by the time she had completed her sentence.

Penelope grinned. "I will use anything he lets me use," she said.

They all laughed again and made intense profusions of astonishment and amusement, and by the time they had all settled back into a quieter enjoyment of one another's company, Penelope was sure that she was blushing fiercely. They spent the next hour or so talking over Penelope's wedding plans, all of them anxious to hear what she had in store for the wedding day. And as she explained it all, she felt happier than she had ever been.

Most of the plans had been sorted out already. She and Odysseus would be married in the local temple of Aphrodite. It would be a short ceremony, and then the reception afterwards would be held at Foxcliff Manor, her new home. It was to be a lavish affair with at least ten different assortments of wine, a few ales, and more food than Penelope had ever seen in one place before. Cheeses and breads would be provided as the first course; there was to be a spring salad of mixed vegetables and fruits for the second course; the cook had planned a sherbet for the third course to cleanse the palate; the fourth course would be baked fish; the fifth course would be roasted pig with parsnips, and lastly there would be at least four different types of cake.

The ladies were shocked and excited, listening to Penelope talk about the menu. Ithaca was known for its celebrations whenever someone of importance was married, and from the sound of it, Penelope and Odysseus' wedding would not disappoint. Indeed, it seemed it would set the new standard for weddings moving forward. But Penelope would divulge no further information, wanting her friends to be as surprised and pleased on the day of as she was already. They all, therefore, finished their tea, said their goodbyes, and went their separate ways.

That evening, Odysseus supped with Penelope and her father, as he did most days. It pleased Penelope to see him making such an effort to get to know her father as well as herself. Lord Auckland was an older man and was not in great health. Penelope saw how much it pleased him to not only welcome Odysseus into his home so often, but to really connect with the duke. It may have started because of her and Odysseus' engagement, but it continued because the two men got on so well. Lord Auckland was fond of hunting, which was why he had ensured Penelope would learn to hunt along with him, but it had been many years since he had been well enough to go on a hunt; instead, he regaled Odysseus with stories from his past and tricks he had learned over his many years as a hunter. Penelope loved watching her father's eyes light up as he recalled his favorite hunting moments, and she equally enjoyed watching Odysseus listen and comment on those stories. It warmed her heart to know that her future husband and her father would be good friends.

CHAPTER SIX

Profound and Unhidden Desire

Wovenspell Abbey,
Perachori, Ithaca
Greece

Odysseus had not been at the Auckland estate for more than an hour before he mentioned a longing for a hunt. Lord Auckland was long past his hunting days, but within moments it was decided that Penelope would accompany Odysseus on his hunt. And in less than an hour, the two of them were mounted on their horses riding into the forest on the Auckland estate.

"I am surprised your father so willingly consented to letting us go hunting on our own," Odysseus said as he mounted his horse. "Especially since you and I are not yet wed."

Penelope grinned, already atop her mount. "I suppose this is his way of saying he trusts you," she said, her bright eyes flashing playfully. "Or perhaps he knows I can handle myself and my rifle excellently and will not be defenseless."

Odysseus looked over his shoulder at her, a look of surprise on his face. But when he saw her playful smirk, he smiled and shook his head. "You, Miss Penelope Auckland, are incorrigible."

She shrugged. "As is my right as a woman, wouldn't you agree?"

She did not wait for him to answer and, instead, spurred her horse into a gallop across the field towards the surrounding woods. Penelope had not been hunting in several months, but she quickly settled back into the feel of riding side saddle and the pounding rhythm of her horse's stride. She prided herself on being an excellent horsewoman, and knew the forests on her father's estate as if she had traversed them as often as her garden. Given the time of year, she hoped they would come across a turkey or two. Bears were also popular in the spring months, but those she hoped not to encounter.

She slowed her horse to a walk as they entered the woods, and soon Odysseus was walking his mount next to hers, his eyes flashing with mischief.

"It is interesting that your father insisted on your learning to hunt," he said, ensuring to keep his voice quiet as they made their way to the glen where Lord Auckland had suggested they start their hunt. "I have never known a woman to be taught to hunt before."

She nodded. "It is strange, to be sure. I cannot even count how many instructors refused to take me on as a pupil at first. Apparently, they thought it would tarnish their reputations as excellent marksmen to train a girl."

Odysseus furrowed his eyebrows. "Why would they think that?"

"They expected I would fail," she said, glancing over at him, "and, therein, would make them look like failures as my instructors."

Odysseus nodded slowly, his brows still furrowed in thought.

"It wasn't until my father found a woman marksman that my instruction began in earnest. Up until then, my father had shown me the proper ways to handle a rifle; how to load it, aim it, and how best to breathe while shooting. I was allowed to practice in the yard, but he wanted me to learn from an actual hunter before trying to hunt on my own."

"Your father hired a woman marksman?" Odysseus asked. "I did not know there were any."

Penelope nodded. "Her name is Arabella Stag. She is the only woman hunter and marksman in Greece, and has received many marks of distinction from King Menelaus."

Odysseus nodded. "Indeed, I have heard of her, now you mention it."

"She cost a small fortune, but her instruction was priceless." She smiled. "I'll never forget my first hunt. Women join men on the hunt quite often, you know, but never with their own attendant and r-ifle. The men laughed at me when they thought I wasn't listening. I promised myself I would make as many shots that day as the best among them. Show them what a woman with a rifle could really do."

Odysseus smiled. "And did you?"

Penelope sighed. "The best hunter that day was the late Lord Cap-shaw," she said, "a man renowned for his hunting abilities. We were hunting pheasants, and he shot four that we were able to confirm."

"Four? That is quite a lot for a group hunt."

Penelope nodded. "Indeed, it is." She turned her face towards Odysseus, beaming brightly. "I shot and killed six."

Odysseus raised his eyebrows. "You out shot Lord Capshaw? Antinous' father? On your first hunt?"

"I did. At fifteen years old, too. He was very good humored about it. Thought it about time someone kept him on his toes. But the real satisfaction came from the reactions of the other hunters, most of whom were the instructors who had refused to teach me."

Odysseus laughed. "I can only imagine the looks on their faces."

"I shall never forget it for as long as I live," she replied, smiling widely, her eyes full of joy at the recollection. "When we returned home, my father was waiting anxiously. He saw my six pheasants and then asked how many pheasants the others had killed. When I told him, his eyes grew bright with pride."

"I am sure he could not have been prouder."

She laughed. "Indeed. He was, however, perturbed when he heard of how the other hunters had initially laughed at me. After hosting a hunting party, he typically invited everyone in for dinner, and that day was no exception. The cook had prepared a delicious meal of roasted ham." She turned and looked at Odysseus, her eyes flashing with joy and amusement. "There were six other hunters that day, besides myself and the late Lord Capshaw. While we were given ham for our dinner, they were given the six pheasants I had killed."

Odysseus raised his eyebrows and let out a half-gasp, half-laugh. "He didn't!"

Penelope nodded. "He did, indeed. And none of them could say anything, even though they knew precisely what it meant." Her eyes filled with tears. "I have never loved my father more than that day."

She met Odysseus' gaze and saw in his eyes a myriad of emotions, but the most prominent was a profound and unhidden desire. Not the look of lust from a man seeking to ravish, as was common, but an admiration and respect that led to passion. Penelope's stomach filled with flutters. She nearly looked away, so intense was his stare, but she, too, held the same desire, the same passion, and wanted him to know it. In truth, the more time they spent together, the harder it became to keep those desires hidden. If she had known how greatly he wanted her in that moment, she would have yielded willingly, offered herself to him as a sign of trust.

They came to the glen and dismounted, tying their horses' reins to a tree branch. Penelope grabbed her rifle and began to walk into the glen when Odysseus grabbed her hand and gently turned her to face him. His lips were on hers the next moment. It was a gentle kiss. She could tell he was holding back the passion, trying to communicate his affections only, but his desire was too great to be withheld. Penelope broke the kiss for only a moment to place her rifle on the grass, and then her lips were pressed against his, her hands cupping each side of his face as his hands wrapped around her waist.

It was new, this heightened sense of carnal desire, but Penelope would have been lying if she said she did not enjoy it. Tingling took over her body, every inch of it, though it also localized to one specific place between her legs that even she had never touched before. It was pleasure and heat and yearning like she had never known. With each kiss, it intensified. In mere moments, she was breathing heavily against him, and he against her. His hands pulled her in as though he couldn't get her close enough, but his hands did not wander, did not explore, did not move from her waist to any other part of her body. She wanted them to. She wanted to feel him against every single inch of her skin, but she wasn't about to say so. She didn't even know how to say what she wanted, what to call it. All she knew was that her entire body burned with aching desire.

It was some time before he broke the kiss and stared down into her face. "Forgive me," he said breathlessly. "I couldn't stop myself from kissing you."

She smiled. "I didn't stop you, did I?" she asked, her voice low and a little raspy.

He smiled softly. "I do not wish to tarnish your reputation, even though we are engaged to be married. But it has been some weeks since I have dreamed of holding you so, and I could not help myself."

Penelope laughed. "Do you think I care about my reputation after that?" she asked. "I loved every moment."

His eyes sparkled and he swallowed nervously. "Did you really?"

She nodded. "I did not want you to stop." She couldn't believe she was saying any of this, and yet she couldn't keep the words back.

"Penelope," he started and then stopped, seemingly uncertain of what to do or say.

Only then did Penelope feel the reality of his desire hard against her thigh. She looked down, unsure of what it was at first, and then, when realization dawned, she gave a mild gasp and looked back up at Odysseus. He blushed furiously.

"Forgive me," he said, moving to back away, but Penelope's hands were on his shoulders and she tightened her grip.

"There is nothing to forgive, My Lord," she said softly.

He swallowed again. "I...I can't...address it unless...well, I'd have...have to go into the woods, I think –"

Penelope shook her head. "You do not need to go into the woods," hoping and praying that she was not being too forward with him. She didn't think he would be upset or offended after he had initiated such a kiss, but what she wanted, what she was about to ask for, was beyond that. And she did not know what he would say or how he would think of her if he knew what she wanted from him at that moment. "I'm right here," she added, lowering her voice to a whisper.

He let out a deep sigh. "Penelope, the gods know that I have wanted nothing more than this for months, but..." He shook his head. "I do not wish to disrespect you."

She smiled. "Can it be disrespectful when I want it as badly as you do?"

He seemed to hesitate. "Do you really?" he asked for the second time. "You're not just saying that because you think I want to hear it?"

She shook her head. "Odysseus, please kiss me again. If you do not, I think I will combust."

He did not need to be asked twice. His lips were against hers again. His arms wrapped around her waist, holding her as close to him as possible. She wrapped her arms around his neck and let out a moan that she didn't even know was in her throat. She ran her fingers through his hair, her heart beating wildly, her chest heaving with each inhale. A moment later, she felt his fingers working slowly to untie the bodice of her riding dress. He broke the kiss and looked down at her, his forehead against hers.

"You are certain?" he asked.

Penelope didn't think she could want him anymore than she already did, but his consistent concern for her desires and her consent were enough to make her mad with passion.

"I am quite certain," she said.

He kissed her again as his hands slowly pulled at the bodice and it fell away from her, crumpling to the ground. She was only in her stay and chemise now and he broke the kiss again to look down at her. He smiled and looked into her face.

"You're the most beautiful sight I have ever seen," he whispered, sliding the loosened stay over her shoulders with the chemise, exposing her entirely naked body.

Penelope dropped her fingers to the front flap of his trousers and began undoing the fastens. Slowly, gently, she reached her hand inside and grasped ahold of him. His arousal was full and hard and warm, and the feeling of her hand around him elicited a groan from Odysseus that made Penelope's body tingle even more. She watched as all control, all discipline, evaporated from his mind and were replaced with lust and passion. In a fluid motion, he grabbed her, laid her onto her back on the ground, and held himself above her. She felt him against her, but he did not enter her. He simply held himself there and waited.

"Are you trying to torture me?" she asked, staring up at him with pleading eyes, every single inch of her skin desperate to feel him within her.

He shook his head. "I do not wish to hurt you. I'm waiting until I can move gently."

"You will not hurt me."

He raised his eyebrows and grinned amusedly. "Trust me, gentle is better."

He did move then, slowly, and as gently as he could. Penelope sucked in a sharp gasp as he slid into her.

"Should I stop?" he asked.

She shook her head, dizzy with desire and pleasure. "No," she said, "no, do not ever stop."

He grinned and continued until he had slid all the way inside of her. He waited a moment and then began to pump softly, rolling his hips to slide and and out. Penelope felt she would burst from ecstasy. She closed her eyes and focused on the incredible feeling of having him inside of her. Heat had built between her legs and something she could only describe as pressure; they worked in tandem to create the pleasure she felt. She moaned. And groaned. And soon all she knew was sheer bliss.

He slid a hand between their two bodies and gently worked his fingertips against the tender flesh between her legs. Waves of pleasure shot through her and she cried out, glad they had gone so far into the woods. They would have been caught otherwise because she could not contain herself, could not quiet herself under the incredible feeling of his fingers.

"Does it still hurt?" he asked.

She shook her head. "No." And it didn't.

His lips pressed against hers and he began to thrust again, his fingers still working gently between her legs. She couldn't describe the sensation she felt as his fingers brushed against her over and over. It was tingling but also urgent, hot and burning, but not in a painful way. There was pressure building from she didn't know where, but with each movement between her legs and each thrust of his body against hers, everything intensified. His eyes stared down into hers and she saw within them everything Odysseus felt, everything he thought but didn't vocalize. There was desire and lust, yes, but also a passion that went beyond the physicality of their union beneath the trees. This wasn't just his lust taking control of his body, it was also a manifestation of his love for her, his need to have her with him in every way.

The next moment, everything that had been building came to a sudden explosion of release. Every muscle in her body clenched and she let out a piercing cry of utter pleasure as the climax rolled over her. Odysseus, too, seemed near to his own release and let out a cry of pleasure mere seconds later.

They laid there for several moments, neither of them able to speak through heavy breathing. Penelope, aware that she had just given herself to Odysseus before they were really married, was far from wishing she could take it back. Under other circumstances or with a different man, her feelings might have been the opposite. But even as she looked over at Odysseus and saw the same love and devotion in his eyes as she had seen the day he proposed, she knew that this moment, this choice, had been no mistake. She had wanted him as much as he had wanted her. She had given herself as much as he had given of himself. And now she knew what kind of love she could expect from her husband on their wedding night, and she could not wait.

"Shall we…try that again soon?" she asked, flashing a teasing smile his way.

"Penelope," he said, smiling widely, still out of breath, "if I thought you were serious, I would already be on top of you."

She chuckled. "Well then, I do not know why you're still all the way over there, Your Grace, because I am quite serious, I assure –" She was cut off by Odysseus' lips pressing to hers once more.

Penelope smiled through the kiss as his hands wandered over her body once again. They would, she realized, likely not get to any hunting that afternoon.

CHAPTER SEVEN

Flutters

Wovenspell Abbey,
Perachori, Ithaca
Greece

Penelope stared at herself in the mirror and felt tears welling in her eyes. It had been a few weeks since Odysseus had proposed and she now stood and stared at herself in her wedding dress. It was the second of what would be three different fittings, but this was the first time she felt like a real bride. The dress was made of fine ivory silk with a beautiful, hand-made lace overlay that matched the lace of her veil. Her smile was wide.

"You are pleased, my lady?" asked Iris, the seamstress.

Penelope nodded. "I am beyond pleased, Iris. You have outdone yourself this time."

"Only the best for our soon-to-be duchess," she replied, continuing to make adjustments with her pins at the hem of the skirt. "He will not know how to contain himself when he sees you walking to the altar, my lady."

Penelope blushed, thinking of the time they had spent "hunting" in the woods only a few days before. She had been worried that his interest in her would fade now that he had known her so intimately, but indeed, the opposite had been true. He had dined with her and her father every evening since then, and the ways he looked at her now held something they hadn't before, something Penelope could only describe as a burning passion.

"Will the dress be ready by the end of April?" Penelope asked.

"Yes, madam. You have my word."

Penelope let out a sigh of contentment and slowly took off the dress. It was already early evening and Odysseus was to dine with them again, as were two of his closest friends, Captain Achilles Lawrence and Lieutenant Patroclus Eliot. Penelope knew of the two men but had never met them. According to Odysseus, they were anxious to make her acquaintance, and Penelope could not deny her equal fervor to meet them as well. She hoped they would approve of her.

"Grace," she said over her shoulder to her lady's maid, "please grab the gold gown for supper tonight," she said.

Grace went to the wardrobe and produced the gown. It was made of shimmering golden muslin trimmed with crimson silk. It was a gown she'd had made some months before Odysseus had expressed his interest, but had never had occasion to wear. It was not quite right for a ball as it was not really a ballgown, but it was much too fancy for her to wear to dinner when it was only her father and her dining. But tonight she wanted to make a strong impression. She would look the role of a duchess.

By the time she had finished changing, it was announced that Odysseus had arrived. Penelope put on her gloves and walked down the stairs where the duke and her father were already chatting in the foyer. Odysseus looked up as she descended the staircase. His eyes locked with hers and never wavered. She smiled, feeling herself blush under the intensity of his stare, but she did not look away.

"Ah, just on time, my dear," said her father.

She curtseyed to greet Odysseus, and he bowed.

"It is good to see you, Your Grace," she said.

"Not as good as it is for me to see you," he replied with a grin.

He held out his arm to her which she took and they walked into the drawing room where tea and refreshments had already been laid out. Supper was not going to be ready for another hour or so. Penelope made up a cup of tea for Odysseus and one for her father before making her own and sitting on the sofa across from the two men.

"I trust you had a fine day, Your Grace?" she asked.

He nodded. "I did. I meet with my tenants twice a month and today was one of those days."

"And how do your tenants fare?" she asked, taking a sip from her tea.

"Exceedingly well. Last year's harvest was bountiful and so the farmers all did very well at the market. In the summer I will be hosting the Ithacan festival to choose which of the farms will be supplying me vegetables, fruits, poultry, and other such foods, so these visits help me to see which farms are doing the best and which might need the extra income."

Penelope grinned. "Will one of them also be chosen to supply necessary foods for the wedding, Your Grace?"

He smiled. "I had not thought of that until now, but what a splendid idea. I could help support more than one of the farms that way." He looked over at Lord Auckland. "Your daughter's intelligence continues to surprise, my lord."

Her father bowed his head thankfully and then flashed a bright smile towards Penelope. Her heart surged, knowing that she was making both men proud. This was what she had been raised to do, but it was one thing to know she could do it and quite another to see that she already was.

Just then, the bell rang, indicating that their other guests had arrived. Penelope's heart surged again, but this time in nervousness. She nearly dropped her cup of tea. She set it on the side table and stood to her feet as the butler went to answer the door. Odysseus moved to step closer to her.

"Do not fret," he said with a gentle smile. "You will be perfect. You always are."

She looked up at him, not quite sure she wanted to be seen as perfect. But there was no time to discuss the matter. Instead, she turned, smiled, and curtseyed as the two officers were brought into the room.

Both men wore their red wool infantry coats. Captain Achilles was a large man; tall, easily over six feet, but also strongly built. He wore his blonde hair pulled back and tied with a black ribbon. His skin was heavily tanned and his dark eyes sparkled with life and enthusiasm. Lieutenant Patroclus was shorter by several inches with short, black curly hair, a fair complexion, and blue eyes.

Both men shook hands with Odysseus first and then Lord Auckland, once the duke had introduced them. Then, all eyes turned towards Penelope and she felt herself begin to tremble.

"And this," Odysseus said, "is my betrothed, the Lady Penelope Auckland."

She curtseyed a second time as they also bowed.

"It is a pleasure," said Achilles, "to meet the woman who has captured this rascal's fancy."

Penelope grinned. "A rascal, you say?"

Achilles nodded. "I have known this man since we were children and I can promise you, whatever pretenses he adorns himself with, he is and will always be a rascal." He winked.

Odysseus sighed. "You are going to give my soon-to-be bride false ideas of me, Achilles."

The man held up his hands, as if absolving himself of any responsibility. "I am merely ensuring the young lady knows what she is in for, that's all."

Penelope turned a curious glance to Odysseus who seemed to be unable to meet her gaze at that moment.

"Do not take anything the Captain says to heart, my lady," said Patroclus, taking a step towards her. "His favorite pastime is embarrassing his friends as profoundly as he is able. Take everything he says with a large grain of salt."

The look of astonishment and offense on Achilles' face was evident.

"You're not supposed to give away the secret, Patroclus. It takes the humor out of it."

Patroclus shook his head. "I'll not be responsible for a dispute between the couple over absolutely nothing at all. Not on our first meeting, at least. We should save that for after the wedding."

Achilles sighed and waved his hand at Patroclus. "It was a mere jest and nothing more. And now you've ruined it."

Penelope laughed then, heartily enjoying the banter. Odysseus smiled at her, but there was still something in his eyes, or rather behind them, that she couldn't quite make out. Whatever the jest had been, it had been based on something true. That much she could ascertain. But she was not really worried. Odysseus was several years older than she and, though she did not know much about the ways and lives of men, she knew that they were granted more privacy and independence than women. Perhaps there was something in his past for which he was not proud, but which was not necessarily shameful either.

"My dear," said Lord Auckland after the guests had all been given their tea, "might you consent to play a song for us?"

Penelope smiled and walked to the piano. There was a special song she had been practicing for just this occasion. It was a song of desire, of newly resonating love between two people. It was beautiful, both passionate and playful, written from the perspective of the woman for her new husband.

She sat at the piano and opened up her music. Slowly, she began to play, her fingers dancing across the keys as she moved through the song. Her voice echoed off the walls of the drawing room, joined only by the sound of the crackling fire in the hearth. As she played, she lifted her gaze to look at Odysseus. He was serious and stern, which she had not expected, but there was a flicker in his eyes that made Penelope's heart flutter.

CHAPTER EIGHT

Given Proper Warning

Odysseus watched as Penelope finished the song. His chest was tight with embarrassment. It wasn't that Achilles had said anything wrong, but rather that Penelope did not know the man well enough to understand his jests. Odysseus had, indeed, been a bit of a rascal in his younger years. Achilles had witnessed some of Odysseus' more adventurous pursuits, and those were moments of his life of which Odysseus, while not embarrassed, was not entirely proud of. It wasn't that he had done wrong or that he wished he had done differently, but rather that he did not know how to explain those things to Penelope. He had not anticipated that Achilles would reference them within the first moments of meeting Penelope, else he would have given her proper warning.

He could tell, too, that Penelope was now on edge. She could hardly meet his gaze after Achilles' words. Not even Patroclus' assurances had been enough to offer comfort, and for that, Odysseus was upset. More so than he needed to be, but he couldn't help it.

"You're scowling," Achilles whispered to him as Penelope finished up her first song and was prevailed upon by both her father and Patroclus to play another, to which she readily acquiesced. "We're celebrating your engagement after all. At least try not to look so angry."

"I am trying," he whispered back in a harsher tone than he intended, "but it is hard when you speak out of turn but bear no responsibility for the consequences of your words."

Achilles sighed. "I am sorry. I was trying not to be too serious. You spoke so highly of her wit and good humor, that I wanted to start the evening playfully. I can remedy the situation at dinner and explain myself, if that would help?"

Odysseus let out a slow breath. "It is not your situation to remedy," he said, "it is mine. Perhaps, though, you can keep references to my past to a minimum?" he asked, glaring at Achilles. "I'd like not to have to explain more than one failing of mine at a time."

"I shall say nothing of you that will embarrass or upset you or your intended," his friend replied, though his tone was sharp, indicating his own discontentment.

Odysseus turned his focus back to Penelope. He smiled as she played, happy to be near her, and hoping that his explanations to her later would be sufficient to put any concerns or fears she had to rest. He loved her, and he hoped she knew that. He had not always behaved as he should as both a noble and a gentleman and, even considering what had transpired between the two of them in the woods, he was not one to play with a woman's virtue. The only other woman he had been so intimate with had been an opera singer he'd known nearly ten years prior, and even that had been no mere dalliance. Indeed, he had intended to marry the girl and, despite the risks to his future and inheritance, had very nearly proposed.

When their relationship had come to an end, the opera singer had not been ruined; it was common for actresses and other such people to be much more liberal with their interactions with members of both the same and opposite sex, and so there had been no expectation of a remedy to scandal. But should anyone discover what had transpired between him and Penelope, there would, indeed, be a scandal, and that Odysseus did not want.

Penelope's eyes glanced his way as she came to the end of her song and she smiled softly, seeing his eyes on her so intently. The bell was rung for dinner then, and so they all made their way out of the drawing room and into the dining room. Odysseus escorted Penelope there behind everyone else, hoping to at least ease her mind with a few words of affection.

"You played beautifully," he said, smiling down into her lovely face, "I hope Achilles did not upset you too much?"

He felt her tense on his arm. She shook her head.

"No, I am not upset," she said smiling, though it did not quite reach her eyes.

Odysseus sighed. "I can give particulars later if you'd like, but I promise there is nothing you need to worry about."

She offered another soft smile and nodded.

"I trust you, Your Grace. You do not need to explain anything."

She sat at the table and Odysseus wished he felt comforted by her words, but he did not. He had never worried about his past before, so he did not know why it bothered him so heavily now. His time with Miss Constance Greene, the opera singer, had been happy and even though he had intended to marry her, the breaking off of their relationship had not been harsh or full of heartbreak. She had been invited to sing for the Royal Opera in Athens, a glorious honor that set her in comfort for the rest of her life. How could he have asked her to give that up? She had, therefore, left Ithaca and he had moved on.

What was there to regret? What was there to be ashamed of? He had done no different than what other men did so often. Nay, he had behaved better for he had not taken advantage of a woman too naive to recognize what he was doing. Indeed, Odysseus felt that he had lived a good and honorable life and could not now determine why he felt guilty.

Dinner was served. It began with a delicious potato leek soup served cold.

"So tell me," said Lord Auckland as they began to eat, "how did you come to be Captain Lawrence's companion, Lieutenant?"

Patroclus looked up from his bowl of soup. His eyes went from Lord Auckland to Achilles and then back again.

"Captain Lawrence picked me, my lord," he said at last, "almost immediately after I took a position in His Majesty's Infantry."

Achilles smiled. "I needed someone dependable, someone I could trust to help me in my duties," he said, smiling tenderly at Patroclus. "It was only a matter of weeks before we were the best of friends."

"You were fortunate to find such a reliable aid so quickly," Penelope said.

Achilles nodded. "Indeed, I was. Although I must say that I feel as though I would have found him eventually, no matter how long it took."

Penelope raised her eyebrows. "Really? Why?"

Achilles and Patroclus shared a long stare before Achilles looked back at Penelope. "Fate, my lady. Our hearts are too entwined to be kept apart."

A heavy silence settled over the table for a moment, and then it faded.

Penelope smiled. "You are a couple, then?" she asked, her eyes sparkling brightly. "Indeed, I do not understand why I did not notice it before, for there is a profound tenderness between the two of you."

Patroclus smiled. "We often try not to be too obvious, in case the company we're with does not approve."

Penelope nodded. "How much society likes to judge what they do not understand," she said. "I am sorry you have to hide or feel that you must diminish your love for one another."

The two men smiled sadly. "It is an unfortunate reality, I am afraid," said Patroclus.

Penelope sighed. "I do not understand what the issue is. You're both adults. You're both consenting to the relationship. And you both love each other. What else should matter?"

"My thoughts precisely, my lady," replied Achilles.

Odysseus felt his heart surge in his chest. He smiled at her tenderly, hoping she could see how pleased he was. He didn't think she could take his breath away any more than she already had, and here she was, surprising him over and over.

"Well, should circumstances allow it and should the two of you decide you want to, you must let me know about the wedding," she said, smiling sincerely. "I will be in attendance and will make sure my closest acquaintances are as well."

The smile on Achilles' face was such that Odysseus had only rarely seen. His eyes were filled with emotion and it was clear the man was holding back tears, which was a profound accomplishment, indeed. Achilles was never emotional in such ways unless particularly touched by something. Odysseus felt he could not be any happier, seeing that the woman he loved and the friends he cared so much for were getting along as well as they were. It was a comfort to his heart to know that they would not merely tolerate one another for his sake, but develop their own friendship and intimacy. It was something Odysseus desired greatly, even if Achilles could put his foot in his own mouth a little too often.

Supper continued in much the same way. The group continued to eat and converse, and it did not take long at all for Achilles and Patroclus and Penelope to become comfortable with one another as if they had always been the best of friends. It did Oyddseus' heart good to see his favorite people in all the world grow close to one another.

CHAPTER NINE

For My Daughter's Sake

April, 13th Century B.C.E.
Aranea Park,
Perichori, Ithaca
Greece

Antinous stepped out of his carriage and looked at the house before him. It was the Webb estate; a comfortable house that was neither large nor grand, but was perfectly respectable. It was situated on a moderate amount of land that brought in close to £1500 each year. Mr. Webb's estate largely revolved around the raising and shearing of sheep. Wool was the primary product sold from the Webb estate, although they did also supply the butcher with lamb and mutton throughout the year. And while there was nothing demeaning about the work, it did fill Antinous with mild disgust. Of all the things to raise on their estate, it had to be sheep.

Antinous had spent some time here in weeks past, and yet this trip made him ill. He felt himself a fool, indeed, for ever having believed the gossip at Pine's Gentleman's Club. He couldn't even remember who it was now, but someone had led him to believe the Webbs were much more prosperous than they let on. Antinous had asked about the size of their estate, believing that it couldn't possibly bring in such a high amount of wealth, and he was told that their fortune had not come from the estate itself but from a sizable inheritance left by a distant relative.

Always desiring to improve his personal wealth, Antinous had immediately called upon Mr. Webb's daughter and paid her as much positive attention as he could. He'd had no real intentions of marrying at that time, but nor did he want to risk losing the chance of winning her affection before anyone else heard of their newfound wealth. Abigail Webb was an only child which meant she would be the sole inheritor of her father's estate and any other fortune left behind. And even if the estate itself weren't worth much, he could still sell it and add to the size of his own account.

It had taken nearly two months before he had been made aware of how greatly he had been deceived. The Webbs were not poor, to be sure, but nor were they wealthy. The rumored inheritance had been a meager £5,000, much less than the £10,000 he had been led to believe. Moreover, Mr. Webb's dowry for his daughter was a meager £5,000 and not a penny more. It was beyond aggravating knowing that he had spent as much time as he had paying court to a woman who could give him so very little. His anger and disappointment had been profound, and that had been when he'd decided to pursue Penelope Auckland instead. Her inheritance would be much larger than Miss Webb's, and as she was the daughter of an Earl, they were of far more equal rank.

It was what he'd wanted.

It was what he still wanted.

And yet, he was here again at Aranea Park, only now he was to propose to Miss Webb. Anger flared in his chest and flowed through his entire body. After Lord Halstead had made his threats, Antinous had made inquiries to determine if they had been idle or if there was merit to them. The answers he found had been less than desirable. The Duke of Ithaca would not have been able to strip Antinous of his land and title himself, but being the best friend of the king, it was extremely likely King Meneleus would do so without much question. And since Antinous was not acquainted with His Majesty, he would have little to no recourse to ingratiate himself to the king and secure his inheritance irrevocably. Alas, there was nothing he could do. He either proposed to Abigail and married her, or risked losing everything.

With a heavy sigh he made his way to the door and knocked. The butler answered and bowed. "Lord Capshaw, please come in."

Antinous stepped into the foyer. "I am here to meet with Mr. Webb. Is he at home?"

"He is, my lord. If you follow me into the drawing room, I'll fetch him from his study."

Antinous did so and sat on one of the sofas. He would ask Mr. Webb for permission to marry Abigail, and then he would make his suit to the young woman and, in less than an hour's time, would be engaged. He hated the idea of every single second of it.

He did not consider himself a particularly special man. He was handsome as men went, but was certainly no Adonis. He was clever enough and could manage his affairs sufficiently, but he was no genius. He was a man of leisure, of pleasure. He did what he must to fulfill his duty as an Earl, and then devoted the rest of his time to the pursuits that most interested him. No, he was not special, but he believed that he deserved the best of everything. It was why he hired the best cook he could find when he inherited his estate; it was why he only dined at the best restaurants in Ithaca and wore the finest clothes. And he had always intended that he would marry as greatly as he could.

Now, he was about to throw himself away at the feet of a woman without a title, without a fortune, and without anything to offer him at all until her father died. When that happened, he guessed that he would likely sell the estate for no more than a total of £15,000. Hardly what he would call advantageous. It was infuriating and if he had been able to tell Lord Halstead his real opinions of the man, he would have done so in their last meeting. But Odysseus was not only a duke with the king's favor, he was also an impeccable shot. Insulting him so would have resulted in a duel, and Antinous knew it would have been the end of him.

He would have to destroy Odysseus another way. It would take time, he knew, and a lot of scheming and patience, but he was determined. He would marry Abigail. He would do his duty by her, as much as it tortured him, and he would wait until the opportunity arose for him to exact his revenge.

"Lord Capshaw," said Mr. Webb as he came into the room. "I was beginning to wonder if we would ever see you again."

The two men bowed in greeting, but Antinous could hear the irritation in Mr. Webb's voice.

"Yes, alas, business has kept me away for longer than I had hoped. But rest assured, your family has been heavy on my mind since last we met," Antinous said, trying to sound as sincere as he could, though he knew his pretense was an obvious one.

Mr. Webb sat down and studied him for a moment. "To what do I owe this honor?" he asked, though it was clear he suspected Antinous' intentions.

"To be blunt, Mr. Webb, I am here to ask your permission to propose to Miss Webb."

Mr. Webb nodded slowly. "I take it Lord Auckland refused the same request you made to him with regards to his daughter, my lord?"

Antinous felt himself flush, though it was not out of embarrassment but of anger. He should have known that word of his short lived pursuit of Penelope Auckland would have gotten around.

"I will not lie to you, Mr. Webb. I did seek Lord Auckland's permission to propose to Miss Auckland, and as you said, he refused it."

Mr. Webb raised his eyebrows. "Is that all you have to say for yourself?"

"It is the truth. But it should not have any bearing on this conversation between you and I."

"How could it not, my lord? You spent some weeks in this house courting my daughter. You charmed her, you wooed her. I do not hesitate to say that you seduced her, if not of body then at least of heart, and then you left without a word or explanation." Mr. Webb leaned forward with his elbows on his knees. "I do not presume to understand why you pursued my daughter if your motive was money, since you must have known that we cannot compete with the likes of Lord Auckland. My only conclusion can be that you hoped to seduce her completely before abandoning her for Lady Penelope, that you realized after all those months of courtship she would not relinquish her virtue to you, and so you went to ask for Lady Penelope's hand. I can only assume that you are here now because you have no other options."

Antinous blinked a few times. He had not anticipated this kind of reaction from Mr. Webb. Indeed, Antinous had assumed his title and fortune would have secured Mr. Webb's consent on their own merits alone. Mr. Webb was a gentleman of no renown whose daughter was now being noticed by a Viscount. He had expected the father to be the easy yes. Now he realized he had misjudged the man.

"I can offer no explanation, Mr. Webb. I can only say that my intentions towards your daughter have always been honorable, I assure you. I was simply caught up in a sudden and unexpected fascination with Lady Penelope and it ran away with me."

Mr. Webb sneered. "Do you expect me to believe that?"

"I do not expect you to believe anything. But it is the truth."

"And why should I give you my consent now, after so much time has passed? Why should I allow you the opportunity of proposing to my daughter? What do you have to give her?"

Antinous raised his eyebrows. "What do I have to give to her? Are you serious?"

The look on Mr. Webb's face showed that he was deadly serious, and angry on top of that.

"Mr. Webb, I do not mean to be impertinent here, but I am a Viscount. I have a large estate and a fortune. If she marries me, she will be a Viscountess. She will live not merely in comfort but in luxury. She will be elevated beyond anything you could ever hope to offer her. You ask me what it is I will give to her as if I am a pauper needing to prove my worth and I find that offensive."

"And I find it repugnant that you think I would give my daughter away to you just because you have a title and money," Mr. Webb replied with passion. "I saw the heartbreak in her when you stopped visiting and writing. I heard her sobs while she locked herself in her room, determined to try and hide them from me. She has changed from the lively, active girl she used to be to a walking, breathing, shell of who she once was. And I'm supposed to be grateful to you simply because you possess a title?"

Antinous sighed, his temper flaring in his chest. "Perhaps you do not understand the ways of noblemen, Mr. Webb, since you aren't one, but I am doing no differently than anyone in my station would. Yes, I think that my station, my title, my wealth, and my ability to keep your daughter in luxury for the rest of her life should be quit e sufficient to satisfy you."

"Well, it does not, my lord," Mr. Webb replied. "Not even a little. Perhaps you do not understand the ways of fathers who love their children since you have none, but I am doing what any good father would. My daughter may not possess great wealth or status, but she is good and devoted and honest. She deserves better than what you've offered her thus far, and if this pathetic excuse of a conversation is really all you can offer, then I will not be giving you my consent."

Antinous was not only angry then, but fearful. He had truly not expected the day to go like this, and now was facing the real possibility that, even in doing as the duke had instructed, he might still lose everything. He could not flatter or argue his way out of this. He had to be sincere. He had to convince Mr. Webb that he was worthy of marrying his daughter, however absurd the notion was. It should have been Mr. Webb convincing him that his daughter was worthy of his attention, yet here he was, forced to reduce himself before this man who was not and never could be his equal.

"Mr. Webb," he said, lowering his voice and doing his utmost to sound humble, "please forgive me. I have been ungracious and rude, and I must apologize. I truly do not mean you or your amiable daughter any disrespect."

"Then what do you mean, my lord?"

"You have asked me what I am offering your daughter, and you want something more than my title and wealth. That is fair enough. I hope you will believe me when I say that I mean to be good to her. She is a gentle soul, and I intend to be tender with her. I will be an active and attentive husband and, when we have our own children, an active and attentive father. I will do my duty by her and ensure that she has everything she needs, and that includes everything she needs from me specifically."

Mr. Webb did not speak, and so Antinous continued. "I cannot say that I am in love with Abigail. I cannot even say I believe in the existence of such things. I view marriage as a transaction, but one that is only made better and more successful when everyone involved is happy. And I do truly desire for your daughter to be happy as my wife. I am committed to that." He, of course, left out that his reasons for that commitment had been thrust upon him against his will.

Mr. Webb sighed. "I am going to be honest with you, my lord; I do not believe a word of what you just said. But my daughter's wellbeing and happiness are of the utmost importance to me and she wants to marry you."

Antinous felt his heart slam in his chest. He dared not hope that this meant he could press his suit to her. Not until Mr. Webb said the words.

"I tried, gods above, how I tried to talk her out of it, but she would not be swayed. Her heart belongs to you and nothing I say or do will change that. I promised her that if you came here and asked for my permission, as long as I was satisfied by your words, I would give you my consent." He paused a moment. "And though I am not satisfied, I cannot deny that there is logic in much of what you say. I especially cannot deny what you say about other noblemen behaving in the same way, for I know they do, and I cannot fault you for following suit, however much I wish you had behaved differently." He sighed and stared at Antinous for a long while. "I must also admit that I appreciate your candidacy. I wish you did love my daughter. It would bring me a great deal of relief if you did, but I am grateful you did not attempt to deceive me by saying you felt more for her than you do. I admire your honesty."

"Do I have your permission then, Mr. Webb?"

"Against my better judgment, yes. Abigail deserves to be happy and if you say you are willing to try and give her that happiness, then you deserve a chance to prove me wrong in my opinions of you." He glared at Antinous then. "And I truly hope you prove me utterly wrong, my lord. For my daughter's sake."

Antinous stood to his feet, surging with relief. "I swear to you, sir, that I will do my best."

They shook hands then and Antinous asked if he could see Abigail. He had won the first round. He was nearly positive he would win the second, and then his future would be secure.

CHAPTER TEN

Chapter 10: Abigail's Greatest Desire

Abigail sat on the sofa in the library, consumed by the book in her hands. Where some fathers restricted their daughters' access to which books they could read, Mr. Webb did not. He thought it a good thing for young women to be well read and knowledgeable. He encouraged Abigail to read as much as possible, and so she did. It was her favorite pastime.

The current book in her hands was a collection of poems that had been written down from a poet who was growing in popularity. The poet was a woman who would recite her poems, either from memory or by creating them in the moment, and someone in attendance, usually a clerk, would write them down and collect them. The poet's name was Sappho and Abigail felt as though the woman had a keen grasp on the beauties and disappointments of love.

Abigail, too, understood those same beauties and disappointments. It had been some weeks since Viscount Antinous Capshaw visited her, and she did not understand why his visits had stopped. They had been so frequent that she had, perhaps too hastily, assumed he was making designs to propose. She had even begun weaving a tapestry for him as a gift; it chronicled the last three generations of his family, ending with him as the current Viscount. She had taken great care to study the genealogy of his family to ensure her accuracy, and had been working for hours, incorporating some of his favorite things into the tapestry. She originally planned on giving it to him as an engagement present. Now, though, having been so long since he'd last called on her, she wondered if she had been mistaken.

She sighed and looked away from the pages. She was still young at twenty years old, and she knew there would be other suitors. But would they make her laugh as Antinous had? Would they spend hours discussing books and trading suggestions, as she and Antinous had done? Would any of the others make her feel as though her very soul had been consumed by flames? These were questions for which she had no answers, but they filled her with sadness. She knew that the connection between her and Antinous had been real. She had seen it in his eyes and heard it in his voice.

Why, then, had his affections changed?

She did not know. Sometimes she tried to convince herself that he was simply staying away until he was ready to propose, but that didn't make sense, even to her. If he had not been ready to take a wife, he would never have courted her to begin with. She hated the uncertainty, the unanswered questions. She wished she could see him, talk to him, unburden herself of all the concerns that circled in her mind.

Just then, the library door opened and the housekeeper entered and bowed.

"The Viscount Capshaw is here, miss," she said.

Abigail stifled the gasp of panic that rose into her throat and stood to her feet. A moment later, the Viscount did, indeed, walk into the library and Abigail felt a myriad of emotions all at once. She was ecstatic and anxious and worried and angry, and she wished so very badly that she had worn her pale yellow satin day dress. It was the most flattering of her day dresses and, she suspected, Antinous' favorite. But he was here and she had not the time to change.

"My Lord, it is a pleasure to see you," she said as she curtsied and tried to keep the many emotions she felt out of her voice. "It has been so long," she added, hoping it would not come across as angry or unhappy. She set down the book of poems and clasped her hands in front of herself.

Antinous bowed and offered a small smile. "Indeed, it has, Miss Webb. You probably believe me to be a rake and a good-for-nothing, after staying away for so long without any word from me." He approached her, his eyes meeting hers for only a few seconds together.

"I must confess, my lord, I was confused at first and then saddened by the loss of your company," she said, allowing herself the opportunity to be honest without imposing judgment onto him. "But I am pleased to see you now, today." She smiled nervously.

He grinned, but did not speak. She invited him to sit and tried to ignore that ever increasing beat of her heart as it threatened to fill her throat and eliminate her ability to speak entirely.

"To what do I owe this honor?" she asked.

"Well, Miss Webb, I am here on a matter of personal business I hope you can assist me with."

The rapid beat of her heart turned to a rush of butterfly's wings in her belly. She dared not believe that this was the moment she had hoped for, and yet she could think of no other matters of personal business that she could help with besides marriage. She told herself to calm down, to wait until she heard him speak the words before getting her hopes up, but it was too late.

"I think you know, Miss Webb, that I have been tending to the affairs my father left behind when he died. Those affairs have kept me incredibly busy of late, but they have also helped me realize that there are things I desire in my life that I do not currently have. One of those things is companionship."

Abigail felt she would burst. This was the moment she had given up hope would ever come.

"The days that I have spent here have been some of the happiest of my life. And I did not realize how much I missed them until business kept me away." He met her gaze then and offered a tender, even if somewhat unaffected, smile. "At night when I am up late rummaging through papers and receipts and financial documents, I find myself missing one person, and wishing she were there with me, and that person is you."

Abigail smiled, tears filling her eyes.

"And so, Miss Webb, I am here to humbly ask if you would do me the greatest honor of consenting to become my wife?"

She could hardly speak for joy. She nodded enthusiastically, wishing she could throw her arms around his neck and embrace him, but she knew better than to display her affections in such a way.

"Yes, my lord. Nothing would make me happier," she said, hoping he could see the earnestness in her eyes and hear it in her voice. "Indeed, I had previously believed your affections did lean in such a direction, but when you stopped calling, I assumed I had been mistaken in your affections for me."

There was a look of hesitation, she thought, in his eyes then, and so she continued.

"But I understand that, as a Viscount, much is expected of you. I can only imagine the many different duties you must see to on a daily basis and I feel utterly foolish to think that I could monopolize all of your time."

He smiled slightly, the look of hesitation fading from his eyes.

"Your father has already granted his permission," he said, standing to his feet. "And so all that is left is for us to choose the date."

He smiled down at her and Abigail felt herself begin to tremble as she, too, stood to her feet. He reached for her hand and she lifted hers to take hold of his. He pressed his lips to her fingers and then said, "I think tomorrow night I shall come by for dinner. Does that sound like an opportune time to discuss the details of the wedding?"

Abigail nodded, smiling as sweetly as she could. Anitnous bowed, then, and abruptly left the room, leaving her alone with her thoughts. She sat back down on the sofa, trying to keep a smile on her face. It had not quite been what she would call a romantic proposal. It was much closer to a business transaction than a conversation of the future between two people in love. But he had proposed after all, something she had not dared to hope for in some time, so surely that counted for something? Indeed it did, but the longer she sat alone in the drawing room, playing over his proposal and the words he spoke, the less satisfied she found herself. He had said nothing of love, though he had implied that he felt strongly for her; he had said nothing of passion or desire, though he had said he'd missed her.

Were these the typical words of men who loved women? She did not know. In fact, she knew very little of men at all. But she couldn't help but feel as though there was something wanting in Antinous' proposal. His words, his feelings, had not ever reached his eyes. He had barely made eye contact with her. Moreover, he had left so quickly after her answer; they had not embraced, they had not spoken to her father, and she had not even had time to invite him to stay for tea before he'd left.

It was very odd, indeed. Slowly, her happiness and excitement faded into bewilderment and confusion. She did not know what she had done to make him leave so swiftly. Abigail had never known him to be one who struggled with words. As she thought back to the nights when he had visited her before and compared his demeanor, his eloquence, and his expressed emotions to those of his marriage proposal, she saw a great deal was different. It was as though he was a completely different man than before. She didn't know what had changed or why, but she saw distinctly that the man who had first sought her favor was no longer the man who had asked for her hand.

They were engaged which, until that moment, had been her heart's greatest desire. Now, she worried it would be her heart's greatest disappointment.

CHAPTER ELEVEN
Towards Her Future

Late April, 13th Century B.C.E.
Wovenspell Abbey,
Perichori, Ithaca,
Greece

Penelope stood in front of the large looking glass and smiled through tears of joy. She felt radiant in her wedding gown. Her hair had been styled up with strands of curls framing her face. Pins with real salt-water pearls had been placed atop her head in such a way as to resemble a circlet. And hanging from the back of her head was a long veil that trained behind her; it was made of hand-sewn lace with small pearls sewn in. She had never felt so beautiful. Nor had she ever felt so nervous.

Her maid, a young woman named Grace, smiled at her through the mirror. "You look lovely, my lady. I'm sure his grace will be delighted."

Penelope smiled. "Yes, I am sure he will."

Medea, one of her bridesmaids, snorted from behind her. "He would be delighted if she wore nothing but her chemise and stockings."

Penelope grinned and laughed and turned to look at her. Persephone and Eurydice, her other two bridesmaids, gasped and made exclamations about how Medea could be so vulgar, but the woman merely smiled all the wider.

"It is His Grace's wedding day! It does not signify what Penelope wears, he's going to imagine her naked all day regardless!" she said, taking a sip from her cup of tea.

Penelope laughed and shook her head, blushing fiercely. None of them knew that she and Odysseus had already laid together. None of them knew that they had even kissed beyond their engagement day. Penelope had nearly confessed all to Persephone over the course of the morning's busyness, but she had bit her tongue. She didn't want to cause a spectacle, and what would they all think of her if they knew? She wasn't ashamed of what they'd done, nor did she regret it. In fact, she had secretly wished for nothing but to do it again. And again. And again. But she did struggle with the realization that, despite her upbringing, she could so easily abandon her principles in the heat of a moment of passion. She struggled with the burning desire to have him inside of her again, for she had not known before that she would not only enjoy those feelings but revel in them. And she struggled with the fact that rather than feeling mortified or ashamed, she instead had been questioning the very standard of purity she had been raised to value and had so quickly discarded when Odysseus' lips had touched her own

Medea, who had been staring at her in the mirror, gasped and squealed. "I think our Duke of Ithaca may have already seen his intended naked," she said, her voice hushed to a whisper but filled with excitement.

Penelope's eyes met hers in surprise and the soon to be duchess turned quickly to face her bridesmaids. "What on earth did you just say?"

Medea raised her eyebrows and was all smiles. "You heard precisely what I said. Now, either deny it outright, or say nothing, and we will know the truth."

Penelope knew not what to say. She refused to deny it outright. That would have been a lie and she was no liar. But she did not wish for them to know the truth, either. In her hesitation and attempt to wrack her brain for any kind of response that would neither confirm nor deny the accusation, but would also satisfy her friends, a long moment of silence passed and the damage was done. Medea squealed again and clapped her hands and stepped forward.

"I was certain that you couldn't possibly be the picture of purity you presented to the world!" she said, taking Penelope's hands in her own. "You are far too interesting for it."

"Medea –" Penelope started, but Persephone and Eurydice were both there pressing her with questions.

"What was it like?"

"Did it hurt?"

"Was it enjoyable?"

"Were you scared?"

"Did you want it?"

"Was he gentle or rough? I've heard some men are rough."

"Yes, I've heard the same."

"I don't want to imagine that he was rough."

"Ladies!" Penelope shouted, her mind spinning with the rush of what she had just unwittingly revealed to her three closest friends. "Please, you are overwhelming me."

All three of them took steps backward and stopped talking. They stared at her with eyes wide with anticipation. She considered what to say and, as they already knew the truth of it, she decided she would not attempt to deny it. Such a choice would be fruitless anyway, as Medea was so keenly attuned to her expressions and tones of voice. How the woman had sniffed out this secret, Penelope didn't think she would ever know.

"Yes," Penelope said, her voice hushed. "Yes, it's true."

They all squealed loudly and began to pepper her with more questions and professions of excitement. She was relieved, at least, that they weren't judging her. It wasn't that she thought they would, but when a woman's value was so irrevocably linked to her reputation, friends of those who had wandered into their lover's bed before marriage could be tainted by association, and that was something Penelope did not wish for them.

"He was not rough or forceful," she added, and they lowered their voices to listen. "Quite the contrary. He asked at every possible moment if I was certain that I wanted to continue, and even after I said yes repeatedly and with enthusiasm, he went slow. He was incredibly gentle." Penelope smiled at the memory as she replayed it over in her mind.

"Do you wish you had waited?" Persephone asked.

Penelope knew her answer immediately. "Not at all. Is that very wicked of me?"

Medea snorted and shook her head. "Wicked? To desire the person you love and are preparing to spend your life with?"

"I agree with Medea," said Eurydice. "Actions taken with love that do not harm someone else can have no wickedness attached to them."

"And besides," interjected Persephone, "at least now you know what you want. So tonight will be even better still."

Penelope blushed. "Alright, I believe that is quite enough."

"We cannot tease her too much," said Medea. "It is her wedding day, after all. But, once she has returned from her honeymoon, we will tease her relentlessly." She looked at Penelope. "You should prepare yourself."

They all laughed heartily. The morning passed swiftly and, before she was really ready, she was in the carriage that was to take her to the Temple of Aphrodite. It seemed only seconds later she was standing at the entrance waiting for her cue to walk down the aisle. Her father stood beside her, his eyes staring down with love. Penelope was trembling with nerves.

"Are you alright, my darling?" he asked.

She nodded. "I am, father. Only nervous, I think."

"Good nervous or...the kind of nervous where you're second guessing your choice?"

"I'm not second guessing anything," she said, smiling up at him. "But it is going to be an enormous change to my daily life. I am going to live in a new house with new servants. I will not see you everyday, as I am used to. It is...a lot of change at once, and I am feeling somewhat overwhelmed, if I'm honest."

Lord Auckland nodded slowly. "You know, I was the nervous one on the day that I married your mother."

Penelope smiled softly. "You were?"

He nodded. "Your mother was so steady and unmovable. It was a trait that aggravated me whenever we fought, but otherwise it was the thing I admired most about her. It didn't matter what situation she faced, she was always steady and prepared. Whereas I was a mess over the littlest things."

"Well, I can see who it is I take after," Penelope teased.

"You are a great deal like me, it is true, but you are not without some of your mother's traits. I think you are steadier than you know. But even if right now you feel nervous or scared, remember that at that altar stands a man who loves and is devoted to you. That, above all else, is what matters."

Penelope considered his words and would have responded, but the harp began to play and the double doors opened. Her heart raced and she nearly turned around and ran away, but then her eyes fell on Odysseus and she smiled through a sudden burst of tears that filled her eyes. He was there, staring at her with pride and anticipation. At the very sight of him, all of her nervousness faded away and she wanted nothing more than to stand at his side. She took her first step. Her father stepped with her. And they made their way down the aisle towards her future.

CHAPTER TWELVE

He Would Worship This Woman

Odysseus stood at the altar in the Temple of Aphrodite. The ceremony was scheduled to begin in only a few moments, but he felt as though he would explode with nerves. He couldn't stand still. He fidgeted with his thumbs and kept making adjustments to his clothes. King Menelaus was there with his wife, Queen Helen. They greeted him warmly upon entering. When Helen walked away to sit among the other guests, Menelaus leaned in close to Odysseus.

"It is not too late yet," he whispered.

Odysseus furrowed his eyebrows. "For?"

"Leaving," he said, nodding his head towards the entrance. "You and I can leave right now if you so wish."

Odysseus frowned. "Are you really trying to convince me to jilt my fiance on our wedding day, Your Majesty?"

Menelaus merely shrugged and took his seat beside his wife. Odysseus let out a deep breath. He spotted the king's brother, Agamemnon, and his wife, Clytemnestra. Odysseus nodded to them and began to fidget with the buttons on his vest. It was only when Achilles stepped forward and placed a hand on his shoulder, that Odysseus realized just how hard his heart was pounding.

"Are you alright, my friend?" Achilles asked quietly.

Odysseus let out a sigh and shook his head. "I'm much more nervous than I thought I'd be," he said. "I do not know why."

Achilles grinned. "You're joining your life with that of another. It's a big step."

Odysseus nodded, but wasn't sure he agreed. "People marry each other everyday. It's commonplace. It's expected. And this is something I want, so why do I feel so...afraid?"

"Because your life is going to change in a way that you've never experienced before, and regardless of what people think of marriage or how common it is, it is still a daunting change of course in people's lives." He stood in front of Odysseus, his eyes full of compassion and kindness. "It is good that you are nervous. It means you recognize, even subconsciously, the importance of this choice. It means you will not squander the chance for happiness you have been given."

Odysseus smiled softly. That was a comforting thought, one he had not considered.

"Let me ask you this: do you love Penelope?"

Odysseus nodded.

"Do you want to spend the rest of your life with her?"

"More than anything."

"Are you happy to be here, now, waiting for the ceremony to begin? And when you think of the future you two will have from this day forward, does it make you happy? Excited? Grateful?"

Odysseus nodded again. "Yes, all of those things, and more."

"Then you are making the right decision. Revel in that. And do not let your nerves distract you from the reality that today is your wedding day. It is a celebration."

"Achilles, if I did not know any better, I'd say you were the priest preparing to marry the two of us," Odysseus said with a wink.

Achilles snorted. "If you insult me like that again, I will not attend your wedding."

"The ceremony is quite literally minutes away," Odysseus said with a smile.

"I care not," Achilles replied, "I will walk down that aisle and out that door and you will not see me again until after your honeymoon."

Odysseus laughed. "Thank you, my friend. Those are the words I needed to hear."

Achilles raised his eyebrows. "My threats to leave? How very strange."

Odysseus rolled his eyes. "You know what I meant."

"I know." A look of mischief passed into his eyes. "And besides, after today, you can bed her as often as you like and no one can bat an eye."

"Shhh," Odysseus said, looking around. "People will hear you!"

"And I'm sure all of your servants will hear the both of you this evening," he said, wagging his eyebrows up and down.

"I'm walking away from you," Odysseus said, turning and taking a few steps back towards the altar.

Achilles was all giggles as he sat back down. Just then, the harpist began to play and Odysseus felt his heart surge up into his throat. The ceremony was beginning. He turned and looked towards the double doors to the temple as they opened. The sight of Penelope stole his breath away. She walked down the aisle holding her father's arm. Her hair was pinned up and she wore a gown of ivory. She was stunning. The smile on her face and the tears in her eyes told him she felt every bit as nervous as did he, and that gave him leave to allow his own emotions to show on his face.

Their eyes locked as she made her way down the aisle, both of them overcome by the beauty of the moment. Once she stood before him and her father took her hand and gave it to Odysseus, he looked down at her and whispered, "You are breathtaking."

She smiled and blushed as a single tear fell down her cheek. They faced the priest who greeted the congregation. He led them through a prayer, and then gave a small speech about love, marriage, and what the commitment of a life together should mean. Odysseus's heart thundered in his chest, his thoughts wandering to what beauties and tragedies their lives might contain from this moment forward. Surely there would be the light and life of children (many of them, he hoped, having always wanted a large family) and of abundance as Ithaca continued to thrive, but there would be trials also. If King Menelaus couldn't find a peaceful solution to end the war with Troy, more of their men would go to battle, fewer and fewer of them would return, and Ithaca would struggle.

Yet, despite the many scenarios playing through his mind, Odysseus found one constant, one immovable force that would keep him grounded, come what may: his love for Penelope and hers for him. In this, he found himself thanking the gods over and over for sending him a woman so strong and caring. She would be an incredible mother and, he knew, an attentive and committed wife. He would live each day by her standard, doing all he could to cherish her, appreciate her, meet her every need and desire. He knew this as he stared down into her face and spoke his vows. He knew it as she stared into his face and spoke hers. He knew it as they leaned forward and pressed their lips together in a passionate kiss, a symbol of their joining lives, as the priest announced that they were, now, in the eyes of their guests and in the sight of Aphrodite, Lord and Lady Halstead, Duke and Duchess of I thaca.

The sanctuary erupted into applause and many happy cheers. The newlyweds faced the crowd of people assembled there and smiled out at them. Odysseus, unable to control himself, grabbed Penelope, pulled her into his arms, and kissed her again, only this kiss was deeper, more passionate, less reverent than the one before. The assembly cheered louder and clapped and laughed. Penelope, too, laughed behind the kiss. Odysseus lifted her into his arms and carried her back down the aisle towards the carriage that awaited them.

They climbed in and it made its way through town towards the Halstead estate. The moment they were concealed inside of the carriage, Odysseus turned to face his new bride. She was smiling at him, beaming, really, and leaned in close.

"You know that I love you, do you not, Odysseus Halstead?" she asked, her voice soft.

He smiled and pressed a kiss to her forehead. "I do, Penelope Halstead. And you will see and feel just how much love I bear for you later tonight," he said, pressing his lips to hers.

She returned the kiss and wrapped her arms around his neck. He allowed his hand to cup one of her breasts as his tongue teased hers. She moaned and pushed herself closer to him, clearly eager for more of his touch, his passion. He had not intended to initiate such a kiss, but with the windows of the carriage covered, he took the liberty of making the most of their few moments of privacy. Slowly, he slid the bare skin of his hand up her neck and softly gripped the back of her head. He slid his tongue slowly into her mouth, his mind full of their one day of passion in the woods. He felt himself growing hard beneath the sheer amount of desire burning through them both, but he knew there was not enough time to act on it. Not now. Not yet.

"We must not be too disheveled for our guests, my love," he said, forcing himself to pull away from her embrace. "It would be unseemly."

Her eyes flashed with more passion and desire than he had previously seen, and she trailed her fingers down his chest.

"Surely they can wait a few extra minutes," she said, leaning close enough to kiss him, but not quite pressing her lips to his. "It is our day, afterall."

Odysseus let out a sharp breath as his arousal continued to heighten. Gods, she smelled exquisite, and he wanted nothing more than to take her right there. "It is our day, my darling, but we have duties. And as we are about to embark on our honeymoon –" He was cut short as Penelope's hand pressed against him in between his legs. He let out a groan, his body overwhelmed by heat and a need to feel himself against her, inside her.

"Are you really telling me you do not wish for me to keep touching you?" she asked, batting her eyes flirtatiously.

He grinned. "I want nothing more in all the world right now."

"Do you consent to my touch, then?" she asked.

He let out a breathless, "Yes," unable to deny either of them what they so clearly desired.

Her fingers worked at the buttons of his trousers. He knew he should stop her, not because it was wrong, but because the ride from the temple to their estate was not a long one and he didn't think there would be time for them to properly make love. But he quickly found that intercourse was not what Penelope had in mind. Once he was free of his trousers, Penelope leaned forward and seemed to be preparing to take him into her mouth.

"Is this alright?" she asked before doing so, looking up at him.

"Yes," he said, his mind reeling with anticipation.

Odysseus let out a loud moan of pleasure as her warm, wet lips wrapped around him and began to suck. "Oh gods above," he said, closing his eyes and letting his head rest against the backboard of the carriage. It felt positively divine as she sucked and teased, taking his whole length in her mouth at times, and then at others keeping only the tip inside of her. He did not know where on earth or how she had learned to do this, but nor did he care. He was simply grateful she had, and that she was willing to pleasure him in such a way.

"Keep...doing...that..." he said as she took all of him in her mouth, sliding up and down along his shaft.

She did as he asked for a minute more and then suddenly stopped and sat upright. He looked at her, his eyes frantic. "No, why did you stop?"

She smiled seductively and her eyes flashed with mischief. "You said we had not the time for such things," she said meekly.

She was teasing him. Torturously. And he loved every second of it.

"Penelope," he said, "please, go back. Keep going. I'm…I'm close." He was aware he was begging, but he cared not. And the look of sheer pleasure on Penelope's face was enough to show him that she was loving this as much as he was.

She moved back down again, but she did not take him in her mouth. She licked and kissed and touched him as softly as she could. He found himself involuntarily moaning and squirming, desperate for her to touch him more, to suck him properly. His moaning turned to whimpers as she continued in that way and he felt he would go mad with anticipation.

"Please," he said, staring at her, his eyes wide and desperate. He felt he would explode any moment if she would just really take him, but she refused. She continued to tease, to giggle and laugh and lick and kiss – everything but the one he most needed to find his release.

And yet, despite his desperation, he found himself loving every bit of it. His head swam with passion and desire, his heart thundered in his chest, and he thought in that moment that there wasn't a single thing he wouldn't do for this woman. She had transformed in his mind from his wife to his seductress, his goddess of love, and he swore to all the gods, real or imagined, that he would devote himself to her forever. And not just in the ways in which he vowed to during their wedding ceremony; he had meant those words, but they now seemed hollow, not enough to fully encapsulate his love and devotion. No, he decided, he would worship this woman, spend every waking moment doing everything he could to keep her happy, to keep her like she was in this m oment.

She finally took him fully, wrapped her lips around him and sucked. He let out a piercing cry of pleasure as his release, which he had been hanging on the edge of for no less than several minutes, finally crested over him. His fingers and toes tingled in the aftermath and he found himself unable to move. Penelope sat up, smiling widely as she used a handkerchief to wipe her face. She giggled as he continued to breathe heavily and buttoned his trousers back up.

"I trust that was satisfying for you, Your Grace?" she asked coyly.

He grinned. "The second that I am free to do so, I'm going to show you just how satisfying that was for me."

CHAPTER THIRTEEN

Welcome Home

Penelope's heart raced in her chest. She had never imagined in her wildest dreams that she would ever have done something like what she just did; she never imagined that she could so thoroughly tease and drive a man wild with passion, or that she would enjoy the act so very much. And yet she couldn't deny that having a man as powerful as Odysseus turn so weak and malleable over something like her mouth around his cock could be so exhilarating. She knew immediately that she wanted to do this again, to try different movements and amounts of pressure to see what best suited his desires. She, too, found herself aching for his touch, wanting nothing more than for him to press himself inside of her.

She had been entirely unprepared for this awakening, and yet these were the thoughts and fantasies she had been obsessed with since they had given themselves to each other in the woods several weeks before.

They had done nothing else like that since. Not until now, on their carriage ride home.

Penelope and Odysseus arrived at Foxcliff Manor only a few minutes later. They climbed out of the carriage and made their way inside, where they were greeted by both the butler and the housekeeper. Everything was ready for the reception, they said, and Odysseus turned to face Penelope.

"Welcome home, my darling," he said, taking her hand. "I hope you will find nothing but happiness here."

"This is where you live," she said, facing him, "and so how could I be anything but happy with you at my side?"

They shared a kiss and then made their way out to the gardens to await the arrival of their guests. The gardens had been decorated with sashes of red and gold, and several tables had been set up with wine and ale. Penelope felt she must be the princess in a fairytale, so beautifully had everything been set. She whispered a prayer of thanks to the gods and smiled as the first of the guests began to arrive. She was also grateful that the weather was surprisingly warm and clear for late April in Ithaca. She made a mental note to leave a sacrifice of thanks in the Temple of Zeus later in the week.

Achilles approached them with Patroclus. They both bowed to the duke and duchess.

"I must say, I am surprised to see you out here so soon," Achilles said.

Penelope grinned. "What do you mean?"

"You were just married," he said, "I would have thought you two incapable of keeping your hands off one another."

Odysseus and Penelope shared a quick glance and a knowing smile. It wasn't subtle enough to be missed by Achilles who immediately gasped.

"Oh my gods," he exclaimed, "already?" He laughed. "Well, shit, color me surprised."

Penelope laughed, but Odysseus looked incredulous. "Achilles, please! Do not speak so around my wife, I beg."

"Odysseus, it is fine," said Penelope. "It is not as though I haven't used my own mouth for the more wild of...conversations," she said with a smile and a wink.

Odysseus blushed and looked away. Patroclus laughed out loud and said, "Well done!" and bowed to Penelope. And Achilles' mouth dropped open. He stared at Penelope for a moment and then looked back at Odysseus.

"Are you aware, Odysseus, that you have married a goddess? Indeed, I now feel it is most important for me to impress upon you the very real abundance you have been blessed with in such a woman." He looked to Penelope. "I must say, Your Grace, I do not think my friend here has earned the love and passions of one such as yourself."

"Achilles," said Patroclus, placing his hand on the man's shoulder, "I do believe that our new duchess is perfectly capable of deciding for herself who is and is not worthy of her."

Penelope smiled. "Thank you, Patroclus."

Achilles nodded. "Indeed, I do not doubt or question that. I do, however, question what this one did," he said, looking at Odysseus, "to deserve such a vivacious and pleasing woman as his wife."

"Perhaps I refrained from fighting you in another life," Odysseus said pointedly, "Something I do not think I will accomplish in this one."

Achilles let the matter settle, but the smirk on his face did not waver. As more guests continued to arrive, the conversation was steered in a different direction, much to Odysseus' satisfaction, it seemed. Nearly twenty minutes later, King Menelaus and Queen Helen arrived. They walked, hand in hand, towards the newly married couple. Penelope curtsied low and Odysseus bowed deeply.

"Stand, the both of you," the king said.

They did as instructed and Menelaus smiled widely at Odysseus.

"I am most happy for you, my friend," he said. "While you and I are not brothers by blood, I count you as one of my closest friends and most trusted confidants. I have long wished for you to find your own felicity in marriage, and it brings my heart great joy to see that you have." He turned his smiling face towards Penelope. "I would normally say that you, my dear, fortunate to have married so well, but everything I have heard of you and observed myself has shown me that it is, in fact, this rascal who is the fortunate one."

Everyone within earshot chuckled at this. Penelope, too, smiled and bowed her head graciously.

"Thank you, Your Majesty. Perhaps we are both fortunate to have found each other," she said, casting a glance at Odysseus who beamed with pride.

King Menelaus clapped Odysseus on the back. "See?" he said. "You're the lucky one, Halstead. I dare say, you will both be very happy. What better occasion to drink and be merry than a wedding between two such people so in love?"

Everyone clapped and the music began playing again. Queen Helen smiled at Penelope and embraced her, placing two soft kisses to each of Penelope's cheeks. The queen was striking with dark brown skin, long raven black hair that hung well below her shoulders in tight spirals, and a gown of lavender muslin trimmed with silver lace.

"I hope you will both come and visit when you've returned from your honeymoon," she said. "I am anxious to be friends with you, so often have I heard you so well spoken of."

"I would be honored, Your Highness," Penelope said with a curtsy, taken aback at the queen's desire to be on more intimate terms with her.

The king and queen walked away and Penelope turned to Odysseus. She could see in his eyes a look of joy and pride, but also of contentment. King Menelaus was Odysseus' long-time friend; his opinion was of great importance to the Duke of Ithaca, so to hear the king lay such praise at Penelope's feet was a mark in her favor, indeed.

It took some time for all of the guests to arrive and greet the happy couple. Servants passed around glasses of different types of wine and set out finger sandwiches to keep everyone satisfied until the celebration commenced in earnest. Penelope was pleased with all of it, feeling herself very lucky to call this place her home and the man standing next to her husband.

Once everyone had arrived, Penelope and Odysseus began the festivities officially by leading the first dance. It was tremendously beautiful, one that began with just the two of them on the dance floor, and then ended with many other couples around them. One dance led to two, and two to three, and before the afternoon had passed into evening, the Halstead reception had turned into something more akin to a ball than a wedding reception. Penelope was delighted. She and Odysseus did not dance every dance, but they danced frequently, glad to not only lead the way for their guests, but also keep spirits high and interests engaged.

Dinner was served two hours after the start of the reception, a whole hour later than planned, though this ended up being a good thing for the cook who had fallen quite behind in her schedule. Cheeses and bread had been served as guests arrived, and they served to keep them satisfied until dinner was served in full. By the time the guests all sat at their tables, the cook had caught up. The spring salad of mixed vegetables and fruits was served first, followed by a citrus sherbet served in crystal glasses. Baked fish was brought out next, carried by the footmen on silver platters decorated with lemon zest and rosemary. It was served with a honey lemon sauce. The largest course was roasted pig with parsnips. The pigs were roasted outside over large fires. Lastly, four different types of cake were cut and served for everyone to eat as much as they desired.

It was an enormous feast and took nearly two hours for everyone to eat. Conversations filled the evening air as the sun began to set. Torches were lit to keep the party from being consumed by the darkness of the waxing night, and as everyone neared the end of their last course, tea was served along with brandy and port wine.

Another round of dancing ensued, although neither Penelope nor Odysseus participated. Instead they walked around to every table and spent time talking with their guests. They were immaterial conversations, idle chatter, but it showed everyone how much the duke and duchess appreciated their presence. Slowly, people began to leave. No one was rushed away and, indeed, as the night grew late, there was a small cluster of guests that remained and continued to drink and chat with the newlyweds. By the time eleven o'clock rolled around, the last of the guests departed, leaving the couple to themselves. All it took from Penelope was one look over her shoulder at her husband and he had her in his arms, carrying her inside the large house and up the grand staircase towards their bedroom.

Chapter Fourteen

Yearning

Odysseus walked into the large bedroom that Penelope hoped they would share. Couples usually didn't sleep in the same bed unless they were attempting to conceive, or if they were marrying for love. And Penelope felt strongly that intense love and passion and respect connected her heart to his. He set her down, a soft smile on his face as he stared into her eyes.

"I know that this is not our first time being intimate, but I hope you will still find it pleasurable," he said, pressing a slow kiss to her lips.

She was breathing deeply and began inexplicably trembling. It wasn't fear, since she already knew what kind of lover he was, and yet she was on the verge of tears. It was unexpected and she tried to calm herself, but she could not. She was too full of every beautiful emotion to contain them all and she felt she would burst with happiness. He broke the kiss and looked down at her with concern.

"Are you alright?" he asked.

She nodded. "I have never before been so happy as I am now," she said breathlessly. "Tonight was splendid and beautiful, and even though I have just spent the whole day celebrating our marriage, I find myself unable to believe that this is truly happening." A tear rolled down her cheek and he used one of his fingers to gently wipe it away. "Women are almost never as fortunate as I have been this day, and I do not know how to process how lucky I am to be married to a man as wonderful as you."

He smiled and shut the bedroom door, clearly unwilling to brook any interruptions as they consummated their marriage. He pressed his forehead against hers as his hands worked their way to the back of her dress and unfastened the buttons.

"You are the most beautiful woman I have ever known," he whispered as the gown slid off of her shoulders and fell into a heap on the floor. "You are intelligent, clever, witty, and honest. Achilles was right – I do not deserve you." Penelope shook her head and was about to speak, but he held a finger to her lips. "I hope that, one day, I will have loved you well enough to deserve you."

Another tear fell down her cheek. She didn't know how he could possibly put her on such a pedestal, and yet she felt the same for him: that he was too good and she hoped that, one day, she would have proven herself worthy of his love and devotion. To her mind, this was a good sign of not only their mutual love and respect, but also of their compatibility. Their love was based on a desire to serve each other; and that, she thought, was no small thing.

He pressed his lips against hers then in a passionate embrace. His arms wrapped around her and pulled her close and she pressed herself against him willingly. Since their first tryst in the woods, she had been able to think of little else but this, had been unable to wish for little else but this. She needed him, his body, his skin, his scent. She needed him to touch her, tease her, love her fully. It was not merely her body that craved this, although the physical desires were enough to make her dizzy. It was also her heart and her soul, her essence, her entire being that needed his entire being. There was something powerful in the joining of one human body with another, something she could not quite name, and yet felt distinctly as his fingers continued to unfasten her stays and the laces of her chemise.

She moved her fingers to undo the buttons of his coat and vest, desperate to feel the warmth of his skin against hers. He had not been naked when they had first laid together, and she had dreamed of what his skin would feel like against her own. With each layer of clothing she removed, her heart raced further, beat faster, pumped more desire into her until she thought she might scream for him to touch her somewhere, anywhere. It didn't matter. She simply needed him, all of him, to be with all of her. The minutes seemed to drag on for eternity, and yet she hardly recalled removing his trousers or his stockings. But there he was, standing before her, naked and staring at her as intensely as she was staring at him.

"May I touch you?" he asked, and her head swam with enthusiasm.

"If you do not touch me now, I think I might attack you," she said with a smile, and that was all the encouragement he needed.

He wrapped his arms around her again and it was as though he was made with lighting, so strongly did her body begin to hum. Their lips joined in a fervent and fevered kiss. He lifted her into his arms again and carried her to the bed where he lay over her. She thought that this was the moment she had been waiting for, the point in time where they would finally join their bodies like they had in the woods. And indeed, his hand slid down in between her legs and she felt the tips of his fingers press into the aching flesh. She let out an involuntary moan as his skin touched hers, and Odysseus, too, moaned.

"Gods, you're already dripping," he said and Penelope felt her stomach fill with flutters.

"I want you," she said, feeling as though she might cry again, but he shook his head.

"Not yet, my love. There is something else I want to give you."

She furrowed her eyebrows in confusion. "A gift? Now? You want to give me a gift now?"

He chuckled at her and stared into her eyes with such tenderness, Penelope felt she would melt.

"You gave me such pleasure in the carriage this afternoon, and with your permission, I would like to give you the same."

It occurred to her then what he had meant, and her body was suddenly ablaze with new passion, new desire. Yes, yes, she wanted that. She wanted it more than anything else. She nodded enthusiastically.

"I take it I have permission?" he asked, his eyes flashing with excitement.

"Yes, you have permission."

"You must tell me if I do something you do not like," he said, "and likewise, you must tell me when I do something that brings you bliss. Do you understand?"

She nodded, breathing heavily and swift, her heart pounding in her chest. He kissed her forehead and then moved downward, trailing kisses along her chest and her belly. She closed her eyes and let herself revel in each touch, each sensation as he explored her with his lips. Her body was not merely her own in this moment for she had chosen to give herself to him willingly, and it was that shift in belonging that only heightened the pleasure in each touch of his skin against hers. By the time he put his face between her thighs and spread her legs wide, she was aching. She felt herself throbbing even under nothing more than his gaze. He looked at her before beginning.

"You are sure?" he asked.

"Yes!" she exclaimed.

She throbbed again, only this time he saw it and grinned. He looked up at her.

"Already? I have not even begun," he said, his voice deep and primal.

Before she could respond, his tongue was against her, warm and soft and wet. The sound its touch against her elicited from her throat was deep and guttural. It wasn't as though she had never climaxed before; she had pleasured herself many times since their first joining, and in the woods, Odysseus had used his fingers and brought her immense pleasure. But this was an altogether different sensation, one she had not anticipated. She was sensitive, but not so much that it was painful, and yet even as her arousal built, the pressure was something akin to pain. No, not pain – it was a need, a yearning deeper than any desire she had known before.

She didn't know how she was supposed to distinguish between what she liked and what she didn't when everything he did felt glorious. He was soft with his movements, tender, his hot breath tingling against her skin. She did notice after a few minutes that he was moving his tongue in different directions; sometimes up and down with the tip, sometimes side to side or diagonal, and they all made her feel as though she would lose control of her body any second. But it wasn't until he moved his tongue in a circle that she gasped and cried out, "That! Oh gods, please do that again!"

She felt him chuckle as his tongue moved in circles around her hardened clitoris. She grabbed hold of the sheets beneath her and closed her eyes. This was it. This was what her body had been yearning for.

"Keep going," she whispered, hardly even aware that she had said anything at all.

She lost all track of time. All she knew was the heat that flowed through her body as he continued to pleasure her. It was several moments before she realized that the pressure was building. It was stronger now, its need more demanding, and with each movement of his tongue, that need grew to something dire, something that felt as though it would fracture her completely.

"Oh gods," she cried, unable to keep the moans behind her throat any longer.

As if he had sensed the sudden rising pleasure within her, he stopped and pulled his face away. She gasped and opened her eyes and looked down at him. He was smiling up at her.

"What...what are you doing?" she asked, confusedly.

"Teasing you," he said, "the way you teased me this morning."

The ache between her legs intensified. She laid her head back onto the pillow and moaned, her body desperate for his touch. She felt him take a finger and slide it incredibly softly against her, his movements agonizingly slow. She was close to a climax, but not quite close enough for these tender caresses to take her over the edge.

"Please," she pleaded, "your tongue again."

He chuckled. "You sound desperate."

She wanted to laugh and cry simultaneously. "I was so close," she murmured.

His tongue returned to her sensitive flesh and she cried out in pleasure. Odysseus seemed motivated by her sounds, and so she let them tumble out of her. The pleasure was even greater now, although she had not thought that possible. Every movement of his tongue sent bolts of passion and urgency throughout her body. She continued to moan as the pressure built again, and again, Odysseus pulled away, refusing to let her climax.

Only this time, waves of pleasure and unmet desire washed over her and her head swam. But he didn't stay away nearly as long, for his tongue was against her again, urging her closer to release. And again he pulled away only to return seconds later. She lost count of how many times he did this, but each one made her more drunk on passion and lust than the one before it. This, too, was meeting a different kind of desire, one she couldn't describe. It was as though he was speaking directly to her body, giving it what it desired in fragments so that the whole would be even more spectacular.

And indeed, as he pressed his tongue against her again and the dire urgency of her body's desires came close to orgasm, she let out one last cry of desperation and begged him not to stop. He did not stop this time. She practically screamed as the release fell over her in wave after wave of pleasure. It was over a minute later before the release finally subsided and the muscles in her body no longer clenched. Her breathing slowed some and her heartbeat returned to a normal rate. She heard Odysseus move but did not open her eyes until she felt him laying atop her once more.

He stared down at her with love, his eyes now filled with his own need for release.

"I love you, Penelope," he said.

"I love you, Odysseus," she replied, her eyelids heavy from the intensity of her climax.

He slid himself inside of her, slowly, gently, and she let out another moan of pleasure. Something about her climax made his erection feel even more glorious.

"'I've wanted this and only this since the day we spent in the woods," she said as he began to rock his thighs back and forth in gentle thrusts.

"Every time I've touched myself since then, I have thought only of that day," he said.

"Show me," she pleaded, "show me how badly you've desired this."

His movements were still gentle, but Penelope needed more. She used her hands on his thighs to pull him into her harder and faster. He gave her a look of concern but she only nodded, reassuring him that she wanted this. Nay, she needed this, desperately.

He did not hold back.

She let out another cry of pleasure as he thrusted into her, his pelvis smacking against hers. Her entire body was alive with heat, a burning fire of love and passion that she hoped would last forever. She never wanted these desires for her husband to fade. She never wanted to lose this, and she hoped he, too, would always feel this way for her.

Minutes turned to hours in their bedroom. Odysseus climaxed once, crying out with pleasure, and yet he did not stop his movements, did not pull himself from inside of her.

"You can...keep going?" she asked as he breathed heavily.

"With you? Absolutely," he said, pressing his lips to hers. "Besides, I want to feel you climax around my cock this time," he said.

Penelope smiled widely, not ready to end their lovemaking. She didn't think she would ever be ready for it to end. It was as though they had been made to do this with one another. Odysseus was still hard and his movements continued, only now he used one of his hands between her legs to stimulate her. Just like he had in the woods. She moaned and squirmed beneath him, desperate for another release and unable to resist the pleasure of his skin against hers.

"Whenever I pleasured myself after that day in the woods," she said, "this is what I imagined."

He raised his eyebrows. "You've touched yourself?"

She nodded.

"How often?"

"What?" she asked, surprised by his question.

"How often have you touched yourself since that day? Tell me."

She blushed furiously and bit her lower lip. "Do you really wish to know?"

"I'm dying to know."

She smiled. "Twice a day."

He raised his eyebrows and a surprised grin lit his face. "Every day?"

"Without fail."

He kissed her deeply and continued to fondle her between her legs. It took only moments before another release rolled over her. Her second climax led to his, and they both let out moans of pleasure in unison. Odysseus laid next to her, breathing heavily, and Penelope rolled onto her side to stare at him. Neither of them spoke. Both felt the rush of sleep coming over them, but before she allowed her eyes to close, she pressed a kiss to his cheek and told him that she loved him with all her heart, and promised that she always would.

CHAPTER FIFTEEN

Someone of No Great Importance

Laketon Place,
Perichori, Ithaca,
Greece

Antinous sat in his study and stared at the small fire in his hearth. It was not a particularly cold evening, and yet a chill had settled over him that morning when he awoke. It was two days after the wedding of Odysseus Halstead and Penelope Auckland. He had attended the wedding ceremony as well as the celebration afterward, and while the wedding had been a grand affair, Antinous had enjoyed none of it.

He had attended alongside his betrothed, Abigail. She had been pleased and captivated by everything – the decorations, Penelope's wedding clothes, the food, the music; nothing went above her notice and Antinous, still angry over what had essentially been blackmail on Odysseus' part, found himself completely unwilling to have a good time. Abigail didn't notice his foul mood until the reception, when he refused to stand up and dance. She had been crestfallen, something that annoyed him, and he had sulked until her father met his gaze across the table.

Not wanting to face unwanted repercussions from her father, Antinous had asked Abigail to dance, though he hated every second. They had eaten the delicious food and he had attempted to socialize, but his mood would not lift and his sourness would not alter. He was immovably determined to have a wretched time, and though he could tell that he was ruining the experience for Abigail, and through her, her father, nothing he did or told himself would change his demeanor or his attitude. The night had ended as badly as it had begun. They were some of the first of the guests to leave. Antinous had escorted Abigail and her father home, and when he attempted to talk with her about how he had behaved, she had walked away from him without saying a word.

The next day he had gone to see her, but she would not receive him, and he was beginning to suspect that she might cancel their engagement. He did not think this overly likely, but she had never refused to see him before, and he did not know what would happen to him, his land, and his title, if she was the one to break the engagement. Would Odysseus see it as her failing? Or would he assume it was Antinous' fault and follow through on his threats anyway? The Viscount had been in a state of anxiety as he turned to walk home and instead had run into Sir Hawthorn Satchel, Ithaca's primary tradesman. Or, at least, he had been until the king had granted him a baronetcy.

Sir Hawthorn Satchel was a pleasant fellow who always seemed to put himself into conversations and circumstances that had nothing to do with him. The man was a gossip and always wore one of only two different pins on his cravat: a green and silver pin of a tortoise, or a golden pin shaped like winged sandals crested in crystals. He was wearing the winged sandals that day and smiled at Antinous as he bowed a greeting.

"Good morning, Viscount," he said, his brown eyes sparkling. He looked at the Webb house behind him. "Ah, back to visiting Miss Webb, I see!" he said with a wink.

"Good morning, but now is not a good time, Satchel," Antinous had said, turning to walk away.

Hawthorn followed. "It is, indeed, a very fine morning," he said. "And how could it not be, considering the splendid beauty of yesterday's wedding."

"You were not there so how would you know it was either splendid or beautiful?" Antinous snapped, uninterested in humoring the man.

"But I was there," Hawthorn said in response, "You even looked right at me, only you seemed out of sorts, so perhaps you didn't notice my presence."

Antinous did not respond.

"I am sure the happy couple is spending their morning enraptured with each other's company," he said, his voice grating on Antinous' thoughts.

"I am sure that I care nothing whatever for what the duke and duchess are doing," Antinous said, wishing that Hawthorn would leave him be.

"I understand there were many broken hearts that looked upon the wedding," Hawthorn said, his voice changing ever so slightly. "Hearts of those who had sought her hand and been rebuffed."

Antinous felt himself bristling at the statement, but forced himself to keep quiet.

"I even recall hearing of one particular marriage proposal which her father rejected most abruptly. A Viscount, I believe it was," Hawthorn said.

Antinous spun and faced him, his eyes wide. "Do you have a point, fiend? Or are you simply bent on further ruining my morning?"

Hawthorn smiled. "My dear Viscount, I mean no offense. I simply wanted to acknowledge the very valid feelings of anyone who might have been rejected so cruelly by Lord Auckland." He leaned forward. "As I understand it, the young lady had long ago decided on marrying the duke and did everything she could to trap him."

"I have not the slightest idea of what you are talking," Antinous said, when really, he was very interested, indeed. Penelope trapped Odysseus? Now that was gossip he intended to hear, though he would never have dared reveal that interest to anyone.

"Well, they are just rumors," Hawthorn said with a shrug, "but it is my understanding that the young lady did, indeed, target the duke as her desired future husband, and she did and said all she needed to win his good opinion. And then, once he had come courting, she...well, perhaps I shouldn't say. They are rumors. Likely entirely baseless."

Antinous sighed heavily. "I care nothing for idle gossip, Sir Satchel. So if you have nothing else to say, might I go about my morning?" He behaved disinterested, but he very much hoped Hawthorn would continue.

"Oh, but you must hear this," the baronet said with enthusiasm. "For once the duke came courting, lady Penelope Auckland, long considered a pure and righteous woman in the community, did everything she could to ensure the duke would marry her."

Antinous shrugged. "And? Is this not the reality of all feminine arts?"

"I mean that she did everything she could to ensure the duke's commitment." Hawthorn winked.

Antinous felt his heart begin to race. "I hope, Sir Satchel, you are not implying that the daughter of an Earl behaved in a manner...unseemly for her station?"

Hawthorn only smiled.

"Do not be coy, sir. Are you accusing the woman of seducing the duke?"

He shrugged. "I really couldn't say. And honestly, my lord Viscount, I think the prattle of gossipers quite beneath you and I." He sighed. "But if I were making such a statement, it would only be because I trust the source. And it would surely be a shame should such information be made public."

Antinous had looked away as he processed what Hawthorn had told him. Penelope Auckland...seductress. It beggared belief. He hardly knew what to think or do or say, and when he turned to thank Hawthorn for the information, the man was gone.

His conversation with Sir Satchel Hawthorn had been a day ago. Now, he sat alone and sighed heavily as he buried his face in his hands. Deep down, he knew he had behaved poorly at the wedding and reception in ways unbecoming of his status, though it pained him to admit it, even if only to himself. It wasn't that he felt his mood had been unwarranted, because he didn't. Nor did he care that he had made Abigail miserable. It was rather simple: he had wanted to marry Penelope and it was upsetting to watch her marry someone else, especially when the man she was marrying was Odysseus Halstead. No, his mood was not the issue.

But he was a Capshaw, and the men in his family didn't pout over the rejections of a woman. Not ever. Yes, he had wanted to marry Penelope and he was very much disappointed that he had not even been given a chance to prove himself to the young woman. But moping at her wedding? Pitying himself while she hardly even noticed he was there? That was unacceptable. His father, gods rest his soul, would have slapped him if he had been alive to witness it.

Indeed, as he sat and stared at the flames before him, he thought of how he wished he had been merry; he wished he had danced and been pleasant and attended to Abigail; he wished he had made more conversation with those around him because then he would have behaved honorably and according to the standards his father had always expected. If he had simply swallowed his disappointment and behaved the right way, he would have shown Abigail, her father, Penelope, and Odysseus that he was strong enough in the knowledge of his own worth not to care about Penelope or her new husband.

No, he thought, shaking his head. No, it wasn't that. Or, at least, it was not only that. He didn't – he couldn't – care about the opinions of those who saw him as an opportunistic rake unworthy of anyone's respect. No, he should have behaved differently so that he could look at himself with satisfaction and pride. Penelope and Odysseus be damned, but he was a man worth respecting, a man worth knowing. He was one man worth a dozen more from his generation, and yet Penelope and Odysseus cast him aside as someone of no great importance.

He stood to his feet and began to pace. As much as he tried to convince himself that he cared nothing for the duke and duchess's good opinion, he knew at once that it was a lie. He cared too much, he told himself, and yet he couldn't help it. Odysseus was the Duke of Ithaca and best friend to the King of Greece. His opinion might as well have been law, so close were he and the king; being on Odysseus's good side was not merely desirable, it was vital. No one advanced through the ranks of society without the king's favor, and no one was in a better position to convince the king to grant that favor than Odysseus. Not even Queen Helen herself had the king's respect as much as the Duke of Ithaca, if the rumors were to be believed. And Antinous had every intention of earning the king's favor somehow.

But that meant he simply must convince Odysseus to see him in a different light, and there was no way for him to do so except by marrying Abigail Webb. The very idea made him groan. There was nothing wrong with the young woman, but she clearly held feelings for him that he simply did not hold for her. He had charmed her when he thought it necessary, and pursued her when he thought it prudent. But she was not rich, and now he was saddled with her. He tried to think of some way out of the engagement that wouldn't make Odysseus furious, but he could think of nothing at all.

He would have to marry the Webb girl.

He told himself that she would worship him. She would yield to him, be molded by him, and give him sons. He told himself that she was a pretty thing, and there were plenty of men who were saddled with ugly wives, so at least he did not have to face that hardship. But she would not make him happy. That much he knew to be true. How could she? Abigail was a typically accomplished young woman with little talent in anything useful, and no personality that he could connect with. She was not witty. She was clever, but only to a point, and usually just stared at him as he talked without adding any of her own thoughts to the conversation. This had been true even when he had believed her wealthy, but at least then there was a reason for him to feign his interest. Now? They would make each other wretched in time and he found himself hoping that she might die of complications in childbirth, leaving him free to remarry.

This, all of it, was Odysseus's fault. He had blackmailed Antinous, forced him into an engagement with a young woman he did not want to marry. It seemed obvious that Antinous, rather than resign himself to this unwanted fate, should do what he could to ruin Odysseus's life in much the same way. And he knew precisely how to do it. Had not Sir Hawthorn Satchel himself given him the ammunition? Penelope was Odysseus's weakness, that was clear to everyone. He began to pace again, his mind reeling with ideas, most of them useless, but all of them pointed him in the direction he needed to go.

He would still marry Abigail. He had to. No one could suspect that he was behind this mischief, not if he was going to be successful, and the only way to keep himself from getting caught was by feigning his own marital bliss. He decided then that he would buy Abigail an enormous bouquet of her favorite flower; he would write her a letter expressing his deepest regrets over how he had behaved at the wedding, and he would beg her to give him a chance to make it up to her. And he would make it up to her, enough so to be convincing of his love and affection. It didn't need to convince everyone, but it certainly had to convince Odysseus, and that meant Antinous had his work cut out for him.

This plan would take time, he knew. Perhaps years, if need be. But he cared not. He wanted this revenge to be complete, and that meant he would have to be patient. He would get no satisfaction if he acted in haste. No, Odysseus would only be defeated when he stood to lose as much as possible. Penelope would be the key to that destruction, and Antinous' hand would be the one to inflict the blow.

Chapter Sixteen

The Viscount

Aranea Park,

Perichori, Ithaca,

Greece

Abigail Webb sat in the parlor and stared out the window at the gray afternoon. She had tried distracting herself with various things over the last few days, unable to keep thoughts of Antinous' horrible behavior at the duke and duchess' wedding out of her mind. She had originally thought she might pour herself into her music; she had been working on composing an original song on the piano forte and considered that it might be just the thing to distract her, but within mere minutes of placing her fingers atop the keys, she had thought of Antinous and lost all focus.

She had then turned to painting and finishing the landscape of her father's favorite tree just outside the east wing of the house, but she and Antinous had spent many moments outside by that tree in his early days of courtship, and so that did not suit. She had tried embroidery. She had tried taking a stroll outside. She had tried mending some of her own dresses. She had even tried making plans for her wedding with Antinous, but there was nothing that erased her embarrassment and shame. All she could think of was how disappointed she was in him.

She knew he had come to visit the day after the wedding, and she had wanted to let him in. She had wanted to hear his apologies and receive his explanations. She had wanted him to make it right, to ease her mind, for the man she had been with at the wedding was not the man she had fallen in love with. Abigail, try as she might, could not reconcile the Viscount who had originally impressed her with his kindness, his cleverness, and his compassion, with the sulking, petulant child who had escorted her to the duke and duchess's wedding. And of all the events to make a fool out of himself, he had chosen the worst one. Her father had seen everything and was now consistently asking her if she really wanted to marry Antinous. Her friends, too, saw how he had treated her, how neglectful he had been, and they asked her why she had told them he was a kind man. She'd had nothing to say to them beyond, "I have never seen him like this before," and while that at least explained her own confusion to them, it did nothing to assuage her embarrassment or her concern for what they would think of her if she did proceed with their engagement.

But she could not bear the idea of breaking off the engagement. For good or ill, she loved Antinous Capshaw. She had witnessed his capacity for kindness, for compassion, for vulnerability, and she refused to believe that it had all been a farce. But nor could she ignore the very real signs of a weak emotional constitution after such unacceptable behavior in so public a place. Her one relief had been that neither the duke nor duchess seemed to notice his behavior, and so at least she was spared that shame.

A knock sounded at the parlor door and the housekeeper entered. She bowed. "Viscount Antinous Capshaw is requesting an audience with you, miss."

Abigail's heart raced. He had come a second time in person to see her. She had expected a letter when she had refused to see him two days ago, and when none had come, she had despaired over any of this ever being put right. But now he was here and she did not know what to do.

"Bring him in, Mrs. Foster," Abigail said, "and please also tell the cook to prepare tea and some sandwiches."

Mrs. Foster nodded. A moment later she brought Viscount Capshaw into the parlor, and then left to pass on the instructions for tea. Abigail curtsied coldly, forcing herself to remain aloof and reserved. She had not behaved badly at the wedding, and therefore she would not be the one begging for answers or forgiveness. Antinous bowed and the look on his face expressed extreme agitation and anxiety.

"I thought of writing to you after you refused to see me the other day," he said, holding his hat in his hands and picking at the stitches nervously. "But I was worried you wouldn't respond, or perhaps wouldn't even read it, and I very much desire you to hear what I have to say."

She motioned for him to come into the room and sit on the sofa opposite her. He did so, his eyebrows furrowed in thought.

"It is not lost on me how very great an apology I owe you." He met her gaze and Abigail forced herself to remain stoic. Yes, he did owe her a very great deal, and she wasn't about to make this easy for him, no matter how much agony she was in herself. "I escorted you to the wedding not only as a guest of the duke and duchess, but also as my future bride, and as such, I should have been attentive and focused and happy. Instead I was sulking and angry." He shook his head. "I have no excuse. But I hope you will believe me when I say that I am profoundly sorry."

Abigail considered his words. There was truth in what he said, but there was something wanting. Something that plucked at her consciousness that told her she needed to press him harder.

"You say you have no excuse, but I sincerely hope you can provide an explanation. As much as I appreciate your attempt at an apology, I feel I cannot really accept it or offer you forgiveness if I do not understand why you behaved the way you did."

He hesitated and she saw a flash of concern in his eyes. Had he really thought she would accept his apology without asking any questions? Without trying to understand? Clearly he had and now would be disappointed, for she intended to get answers. She waited for a moment to give him a chance to collect his words, and when he did not speak, she met his gaze.

"Surely I am owed more than merely an apology without any context?" she said, her voice sounding much more disinterested than she was. Inwardly, she was miserable. She wanted to reach out and take his hand and offer him her forgiveness. In fact, she was ready to do exactly that, but she could not until she understood precisely what had made him behave in such a way. "If we are to be married, surely I deserve to understand what it is I should expect from my husband-to-be in our daily life? Is this something which I should expect to be a common occurrence?"

He shook his head. "No, of course not."

"And why should I believe that?" He seemed at a loss, and so she kept going. "I have never seen you behave this way before, but it is not the first time you have behaved in a way that has given me cause for concern." He frowned as though confused. "The first being when you suddenly stopped paying court to me after weeks of making your intentions quite clear."

His shoulders slumped and he looked down at his feet. "I thought we had discussed that already?"

"We had. And had you behaved respectably at the wedding as befits your station, I would not now bring it up again. But I am beginning to see a pattern of concerning behavior from you, Antinous, and it does not instill confidence."

"I suppose that is a fair way to look at it," he said, his voice tight and strained.

"It is the only way to look at it from where I sit. Without an explanation from you, I do not know how else I am to see it."

"Are you telling me that you are calling off our engagement?" he asked suddenly.

"Do you wish to call off our engagement?" she countered.

"I wish to do whatever it is I must to regain your trust."

"Then tell me why," she said, keeping her voice calm but showing him enough emotion that he could see she was upset and confused and hurt. "Because if you think me ignorant of the rumors I have heard since our engagement, you are sorely mistaken."

He furrowed his brows. "Rumors? What rumors?"

"That there was a time in recent months that you sought the hand of Lady Penelope yourself and were rejected, and that is why you behaved the way you did at their wedding." His face went pale and she felt as though she had landed on the truth. "Then it is true," she said, turning to look out the window. "I was not your first choice."

She was uncomfortable with the lie she had just told, but she had to know the truth. She had heard that other men besides Odysseus had proposed to Penelope, and she had heard some chatter about a Viscount being among them, but she had heard no names. And until the wedding, she'd had no reason whatsoever to believe Antinous had been one of those men. After the wedding, however, she had been unable to think of any justifiable reason for Antinous' behaviors and, considering how often Abigail found him staring at Penelope, the thought had occurred to her several times. She knew he would have denied it had she asked him outright, and so she had lied and said it was a rumor to see if he would deny it. He had not. And that was as good as admitting it openly.

"Abigail," he said, calling her attention away from the window.

Tears stung her eyes but she refused to let them fall. She looked at him, feeling as though everything she had believed about this man was a lie. He had paid her such kind attentions, and now she knew it was merely him attempting to soothe his heart broken by another woman. And what a woman, indeed! How could she ever compare to the new Duchess of Ithaca? If Antinous' designs had originally been for Lady Penelope, then what could Abigail ever offer him that could meet those expectations?

Antinous moved over to sit next to her. "There was a time when I thought of Penelope as a desirable companion for my future, but it was short lived. I never even got the chance to propose to her, because her father turned me down instantly."

"Did you love her?" Abigail asked, fighting hard to hold back her tears.

He shook his head. "No. She is a beautiful woman, to be sure, and extremely talented in so many ways, but no. I pursued her for her dowry, the fortune she would have inherited, and the opportunity to advance myself in society."

Abigail stared at him incredulously. "You pursued her purely for money and social gain?"

He nodded. "And her father knew it at once and refused his permission outright. It was a passing fancy that meant nothing. I was doing what I had been raised to do. Nothing more. I did not even consider it a matter of honor until her father set me down."

She raised her eyebrows. "He set you down? Truly?"

Antinous nodded. "Quite brashly, if I am being honest, but it is precisely what I needed to hear to recognize that I shouldn't view marriage as a financial transaction. His words, his criticisms, helped me see that marrying for love or even for friendship was a much better choice than seeking to climb the social ladder."

"If that is true, then why did you behave so despicably at their wedding? If, indeed, you never held affection for her, then why?" She felt her heart pounding in her chest. Her resolve was weakening with every word he spoke, but she knew she couldn't give in until he had given her the answers she sought.

He sighed. "I was jealous," he said. "It is a weakness that I have long fought to overcome, but it is something with which I still struggle. I truly care nothing for Lady Penelope aside from what one of her subjects should feel for a duchess, but seeing just how happy she was with Odysseus made me jealous. It was beneath me to feel that way, but no matter how hard I tried to force myself into a better mood, it worsened."

"What were you jealous of?" she asked. "The wedding? The attention? The attendance of the king and queen? For we may not have the king and queen at our wedding, but we will have everyone's attention, too. We will have decorations and splendid food."

He shook his head. "No, it is not that. I'm not even sure I can point to what it was specifically, but from the moment we walked into the temple, I felt an overwhelming amount of jealousy and I could not shake it." He sighed. "This...affliction, or whatever it is, has run in my family a long time. My father and all of my brothers struggled with it. My father's father struggled with it. It is a generational curse, it seems, brought on sometimes by nothing at all." He looked at her, his eyes soft and kind. "I cannot tell you how sorry I am. It was shameful, and you deserved so much better than I was able to offer. I cannot take back what happened, but I can promise to do whatever I can to ensure this state of mind never affects me in such a way again."

Abigail's thoughts ran wild in her mind. She had not considered an affliction of the mind, although she had certainly heard of such things before. She stood to her feet just as tea was brought into the room and began to pace slowly. She did not know if she fully believed Antinous' explanation, and yet the more she considered it, the more she thought it was likely the truth. It was well known that the previous

Viscount had moods as unpredictable as the weather. She had never before considered it might have also passed to his sons.

She faced Antinous. "I believe you," she said. "And I accept your apology."

His eyes brightened. "Truly, my darling?"

She nodded. "And I do not wish to call off our engagement, but I think it would be wise if we implemented a longer engagement than we had originally discussed."

He nodded slowly. "If you think that is necessary..."

"I do. I do not wish for either of us to rush into this marriage without fully understanding what to expect from one another, and I think we need more time to become acquainted with our respective personalities and desires and hopes. What say you?"

He stood to his feet. "I will do anything you ask of me to prove to you how devoted I am to this marriage."

"Very well. Then we will postpone our wedding for now and spend the next few months getting to know each other better."

They both smiled. That, she felt, was a good sign. It was not common for a man of Antinous' status to take orders from others, especially not orders from a woman of no rank. Time, of course, would prove him to be sincere or not, and she intended to pay very close attention to everything he said and did from now on. She would not be humiliated again.

"Will you stay for luncheon with my father and I?" she asked.

He nodded. "I would be delighted."

CHAPTER SEVENTEEN

Settled Back at Foxcliff Manor

Mid-May, 13th Century B.C.E.
Foxcliff Manor,
Perichor, Ithaca
Greece

The wedding had taken place in April and the duke and duchess had spent three weeks in their home with one another. Twice Achilles and Patroclus had been invited to dine with them, and twice Penelope had invited her closest friends to tea, but aside from that, the couple was neither seen nor heard from for a fortnight.

After their honeymoon, the couple began attending plays and operas and orchestral performances in Vathi, the island's most populated city. There were also festivals and concerts among the common folk where the duke and duchess were desired as the most distinguished of guests. Penelope visited orphanages and hospitals to perform charity work, and Odysseus met with local businessmen and discussed the financial issues they were facing.

When they did finally settle back into daily life at Foxcliff Manor, they were no less busy. Odysseus frequently had to meet with his tenants and farmers. He felt it his duty to not only see to the success of his tenants for his sake, but also for their own; if they succeeded, the estate succeeded, thereby making Odysseus a proud and accomplished landlord. Yet, he knew too that it wasn't merely the money that made his estate successful, but the people living on it. His father had impressed upon him the importance of happy tenants who were paid well for their labors.

Odysseus had taken this to heart and, while he expected much from his tenants, he was a fair and reasonable landlord who refused to charge any of his tenants more than they could afford. While some noblemen and landed gentry took no issue evicting tenants who struggled to pay their rent, Odysseus preferred to renegotiate the terms of their lease; he even went so far as to negate the rent to those tenants who struggled more than others to help them reach a place of stability. If he evicted them, there would be no rent coming in anyway; it was better to lose the few pounds he made from their rent and keep them working the land.

While Odysseus worked on his estate with his steward, Penelope paid visits to the tenants herself. She wanted them to know her as well as they knew Odysseus. When she wasn't visiting tenants or seeing to the management of the house, Penelope was entertaining. She hosted several luncheons and invited all of the noble women in Ithaca. She received letters from some of the common folk asking if she would employ their son or daughter, and she responded to all of the letters as promptly as possible. It kept her busy, indeed, and often left her no time to read, garden, or practice shooting. But whatever she felt she had to sacrifice in those moments, she knew would pay out dividends as time went on. She was a duchess, after all, and no longer an Earl's only daughter. Much was expected of her.

Two weeks passed in this way, and Odysseus and Penelope were happy. They would breakfast together in the morning, go about their daily duties, meet together for supper in the evening, and then spend the rest of their night wrapped in each other's embrace. Neither of them had ever imagined they could be so happy, and yet as each day passed, they became more and more content.

"I heard from Baroness Harriet Calf today that there are rumors the king will not sign the treaty with Troy," Penelope said to Odysseus one evening at supper.

Odysseus shook his head as he cut into his slice of roasted beef. "Menelaus is a stubborn, prideful man. He will not sign anything with Troy that does not mostly benefit him."

"His father refused to sign a treaty too," Penelope added, "so it is not surprising that he follows in that man's footsteps."

Odysseus grunted. "Not surprising, no. But it is damned foolish."

Penelope looked up at her husband who sat across the table from her. He sounded angry. "Are you alright, my love?"

He shook his head. "No. I am not. I have lost yet another apprentice studying under Baxter, my steward. He was called in to take up arms in the war."

"What? You do not mean Frederick?" Penelope asked, her heart racing a little faster in her chest.

"I'm afraid I do mean Frederick."

"But he is not even fifteen years old! Nor is he a soldier!"

"I know," Odysseus said, taking another bite. "And yet he has been called away." He shook his head. "He is the fifth such apprentice I have lost. Baxter is a fabulous steward, but he is getting very old. I need someone here to learn how he runs this estate, but how can I give him such a person if that young man will only be called away to war after a few months?"

"What if you brought on a woman to train under Baxter?" Penelope asked, taking a bite of her roasted beef.

Odysseus lifted his gaze and met hers. "You are joking, surely?"

Penelope shook her head. "Not at all. If the issue is that all of our young men keep getting called away to war, then the solution must be that either the king signs a treaty and stops the war altogether, eliminating the issue in the first place, or we adapt and hire an apprentice who will not be called to fight."

Odysseus set down his knife and fork and leaned back in his chair. "Such a thing has never been done before," he said.

Penelope shrugged. "And until my father hired a marksman to teach me to shoot, hunting was exclusively a sport dominated by men." She smiled. "All it takes is for one person to decide that these roles divided among genders are pointless, and then real change happens."

Her husband did not look convinced, though he did not immediately dismiss the idea. "It would be grueling work," he said.

Penelope raised her eyebrows. "Do you think women as a species are incapable of grueling work? I know of four widows who live on your estate who run the farms their husband's left behind. Two of them do so with only one child old enough to help them, and they manage to rear their youngest children at the same time."

Odysseus smiled. "Mrs. Halstead, are you attempting to use the tenants of my own estate against me?"

Penelope's eyes flashed with glee and mischief. "Not against you, Your Grace. Not unless you're determined to argue with me in this matter."

"Whoever the young woman is," Odysseus said, "she would not be given any leniency for being a girl. Baxter is not a tyrant, but he is a hard worker and will expect any apprentice of his to listen to everything he says."

"That would be made clear to anyone applying for the position, regardless of gender," Penelope said, taking a sip of wine.

Odysseus nodded slowly. "It could work," he said. "I'm not sure if Baxter would be on board, but he would be pleased to have consistent help. I know he is tired of starting over every few months when more fighters are needed at the front."

Penelope felt herself growing giddy. "Then...you'll consider it? You'll talk with him about hiring a female apprentice?"

He shook his head. "No, I'll not consider it. I've already made up my mind. We need an apprentice badly, and your idea is the only one which actually provides a solution. We cannot keep hiring young men knowing that they will get called off to war. But, we will be intentional in the kind of woman we hire for such a position. It may be unprecedented, but that is a standard we will set very high, indeed."

Penelope could have squealed, she was so excited. She had wanted to suggest to Odysseus that they consider hiring women for less domestic positions. If men could work inside the house as footmen, underbutlers, and butlers, as well as work out of doors as gardeners, farmers, stewards, and chauffeurs, then women could, likewise, work inside or outside of the house. And if some women were allowed to manage their own farms, then why couldn't other women learn to manage an estate?

"I thought it would also be a good idea to host a ball," Penelope said, cutting into her roasted carrots and radishes. "I'd like to purchase as much local produce and meat as I can, and if we were to host a ball, it would mean I could put more money back in the pockets of those who most depend on us."

Odysseus raised his eyebrows. "You know that we are not the only house who purchases produce from our farms, do you not? Plenty of people from the village buy our produce and dairy and meat."

She nodded. "I know, but I thought it would be a nice surprise if I were to purchase more than what we need for our weekly stores. And it is often the custom that the new couple hosts a ball within the first few months of their wedding as a means of celebrating with the local community. Our wedding held many guests of noble rank, but few of the landed gentry were there, and I should like to host a celebration for them to attend as well."

Her husband grinned. "That is a splendid idea," he said, standing up from the table and walking over to her. "Are you done eating?"

Penelope smiled knowingly and nodded. "Yes, Your Grace. I believe I am done with this roast beef." She stood to her feet and looked up into his face. "Although there is something else I would like to put in my mouth, if that sounds suitable to you?"

He said nothing. He merely pressed his lips to hers, lifted her into his arms, and carried her up the stairs to their bedroom. By this point, all of the house staff knew that the duke and duchess did not merely love each other in the ways that most other noble couples loved their spouse. This was not a pretense. No, the duke and duchess of Ithaca were passionately, deeply in love with one another. They were intimate nearly every day, sometimes more than once a day, and this brought the staff great joy. It meant the duke and duchess would soon celebrate the arrival of a baby. And as Odysseus and Penelope joined themselves in intercourse that evening, there were many of the Foxcliff staff who whispered prayers to the goddess Hera to bless the estate with an heir.

Chapter Eighteen

Who She Was Born to Be

Late-May, 13th Century B.C.E.

Foxcliff Manor,

Perichori, Ithaca,

Greece

The ball was scheduled for a fortnight following and preparations were immediately underway. Penelope oversaw the planning of every aspect of the ball. She met with the cook and went over the menu, choosing each course as carefully as possible. These guests, while not nobility, were, in Penelope's mind, no less important. She did not want any of them to feel slighted by something as seemingly insignificant as what kind of meat and fish were served. She met with the housekeeper and discussed the decorations. Her and Odysseus's wedding reception had been held out of doors due to the sheer number of guests, but the ball would be inside. She, therefore, wanted the decorations to be sublime. Candles, sashes of green and yellow and gold, and flowers were all to be utilized to great effect.

The weeks passed swiftly and, before either of them knew it, the night of the ball had come. Many hundreds of invitations had been sent, though less than half of those invited would actually attend. Penelope wore a gown of white satin trimmed in scarlet and gold. She and Odysseus greeted each of their guests as they arrived. Most of them she knew, but there were some who were new to her.

A handsome man with dark skin and bright blue eyes entered the foyer and Penelope curtsied to greet him. He wore a brilliant pin shaped like a lightning bolt on his cravat.

"Ah, Penelope, this is Baron Zachary Thunderstone," Odysseus said, bowing to the gentleman and then shaking his hand. "He has an estate close to here, but he also helps to manage Deverell Pine's club in Vathi."

"Ah, indeed, it is a pleasure to make your acquaintance, Baron," Penelope said with a smile. "I have heard of that club before. My husband enjoys his evenings at Pine's immensely."

The man smiled and gave a nod. "Thank you, your ladyship. I will pass on the praise to Mr. Pine."

"It is generous of you to give your time to help him manage the club," she said as more guests arrived.

Zachary shrugged. "He is a dear friend and he needs the help. The club is practically overflowing with guests every night."

"Well, you are very welcome here, Baron. Please enjoy yourself."

One after the other, the guests arrived. Odysseus then escorted Penelope into the ballroom where they began the dancing. Other couples soon joined them on the dance floor.

"Will you play and sing for everyone later?" Odysseus asked. "Over supper, perhaps?"

Penelope grinned. "I was already planning on it. I've prepared a special song for the occasion."

Odysseus raised his eyebrows. "Indeed? Well, I am intrigued, Mrs. Halstead."

"I do believe you meant Lady Halstead, or perhaps Your Grace," she said with a wink.

"It is unseemly for a woman of your status to flirt so blatantly with a man in public," he said, leaning in close to whisper in her ear as they spun around each other. "It would be scandalous if someone were to see."

"Well," she said, puffing out her chest ever so slightly to attract his gaze. It worked and he looked down the bodice of her dress. "Then I suppose we shall have a scandal this evening."

The dance took her down the line with another man and away from Odysseus for a moment, but Penelope flashed him a seductive smile as she passed by him. She had never felt so powerful before, and though she knew Odysseus's feelings stemmed from his love for her, she thoroughly enjoyed driving him wild with passion. For a man who was always so in control of himself, it was obvious to everyone that Penelope was, indeed, his one and only weakness. And while she knew his love for her was, in no way, actual weakness, it did make her giddy to see how much of an effect she had on him.

The dance ended and the two hosts moved off of the dance floor and mingled with the guests around them. The first of these Penelope went over to was Abigail Webb, a young woman Penelope had heard a great deal of in recent weeks. Miss Webb was someone Penelope desired to know, seeing as her father was rumored to be given the title of baron soon, so she asked one of the other gentlewomen she already knew to introduce them.

"Thank you for attending our ball, Miss Webb," Penelope said. "I was most looking forward to meeting you at last."

The young woman raised her eyebrows. "At last, Your Grace?"

"Well, I only mean that I have heard your name spoken by many around town as being not only an accomplished young woman, but one very likely to make an advantageous match for yourself." She smiled. "Are you here to find a potential husband, perhaps?"

Abigail smiled and let out a nervous chuckle. "No, indeed, madam. I am actually already engaged, although we have not yet announced it publicly."

"Oh?" Penelope raised one eyebrow. "Why have you not announced it?"

Abigail seemed to hesitate and Penelope realized she had asked something out of turn. She shook her head. "No, do not answer that. I am terribly sorry, Miss Webb. That was impertinent of me."

The young woman smiled sweetly. "No need to apologize, Your Grace. It was a complicated courtship and we are determined not to rush. Waiting for the right time. That is all."

Penelope nodded. "Of course. That makes a great deal of sense. Well, let me be the first to congratulate you now. I take it your intended is not here?"

"No, he had to go into Stavros on a matter of business."

"Well, I hope you will enjoy yourself tonight. In a few weeks, when life here has settled somewhat, I would love for us to have tea and get to know each other better."

Miss Webb raised her eyebrows and blinked, seemingly surprised beyond words.

"I..Thank you, Your Grace," she said with a curtsey. "I would be honored. But, surely, there are other young women more worthy of your time and attention?"

"I do not like ranking women against each other," Penelope replied. "And besides, it is not duty which compels me, but a sincere desire for us to be friends."

Miss Webb smiled. "You are too good, Your Grace. But I will come the moment I am summoned."

"Good. Please, enjoy the evening. And if you want me to find you a dancing partner, let me know."

Penelope walked away, determined that she would get to know more of that young woman. She was kind and caring and well mannered, but there was something else about her that Penelope liked. A kind of openness, an authenticity that Penelope had not often encountered in most people. It was a refreshing change to the stuffy attitudes of most of the noblewomen who had attended her wedding, and she intended to make friends with Abigail. The young woman seemed to her a kindred spirit and she wanted the two of them to be friends. She also resolved to figure out which gentleman she was engaged to. Penelope was curious, indeed. Something gnawed at the back of her mind, as though she already knew who Miss Webb's betrothed was and simply couldn't place the name. She would be sure to make inquiries later.

After some hours of dancing, the music ceased and everyone was ushered into the grand dining hall for dinner. The tables had been decorated vibrantly and everyone was given a specific place to sit.

Penelope and Odysseus both thanked the guests for celebrating with them. Although the ball was not strictly in celebration of their wedding, the festivities and decorations bespoke the trappings of a new husband and wife.

Dinner was served, and it was grand. They began with a delicious leek and potato soup that was served with a light and refreshing white wine. The next course was a cucumber salad with a citrus glaze to cleanse the palette; it was served with champagne. The third course was a tray of oysters and a cut of cod baked with dill and lemon served with a glass of dry white wine. The fourth course was roasted partridge (each guest was given a whole partridge to themselves) served over roasted asparagus and boiled potatoes. The last course was a light desert of raw strawberries with sweet cream.

Dinner lasted some time as the guests mingled and talked amongst themselves. Odysseus smiled at Penelope from where he sat across from her at the head table. The time came for her to play for them all, and so she stood and walked to the grand piano forte. She had, indeed, been preparing her own song for the occasion, and one dedicated specifically to her husband. The lyrics spoke of a young woman longing for a man to love her as truly as she loved herself; and in her search, she finds a man who could have been a god for how loving and gentle and honest he was, and in the end, the couple are married and they live out their days in everlasting affection and respect.

As she played, her eyes continually flitted up to meet Odysseus' and every time she found him staring at her with an intense look of passion and desire and pride. It made her heart flutter to think that she brought him such happiness. And, indeed, she felt like the luckiest woman alive when she thought of all the ways he made her happy.

She lacked nothing. She wanted nothing. He had not only provided her with security and a position, but also more love than she had ever dared hope for. She knew perfectly well that most women could not marry for love, let alone try to find a love match. And so, as she came to the end of her tune, she silently thanked the gods for granting her this blessing that had changed the course of her entire life forever.

Everyone clapped and asked her to play again, and so she did, this time playing a more upbeat song. It was playful and told the tale of a young girl's first experience with love. It was not an original creation like her first song had been, and many of the guests seemed to know it as she played. She finished it quickly and denied requests to play a third. Although she loved music, she was not fond of performing. It made her nervous and she felt that if she played for too long, she would be seen as self-centered. Many people over the years had assured her that this could never be the case as everyone genuinely wanted to hear her play, but she was steadfast: two songs and that was their lot.

But as she returned to her seat and the guests continued to mingle, she couldn't help but feel proud of herself. Not for how well she had played the song, for that was a mere trifle, but for how well she had planned the ball itself. The guests were happy and enjoying themselves. The food was delicious. The orchestra played excellently. It had been a fortnight of planning and rushing and organizing and managing, and all of it had come together seamlessly. It was a mark in her favor as a duchess that this was what she was born to do; this was who she was born to be.

CHAPTER NINETEEN

The Gods Give and the Gods Take Away

Odysseus stared at his wife as she walked back to her seat. His heart swelled with pride. He had known when he first asked her to marry him that she would be an excellent wife. He had known she would be a wonderful manager of the household. He had known that she would be an incredible duchess. But seeing all of these things come to life before him was something he still could not quite process. Everything she did and said was perfect. He really did not feel as though he had done anything to even half-way deserve this woman, and he thanked the gods for granting him such an extraordinary blessing.

In fact, as he watched her, he wondered how he could have ever not felt for her the love he did now. Even when he had asked her to marry him, he had believed himself merely in the process of falling in love, but not quite in love yet. Now, that seemed to be absurd to him. As he thought over the few months they had known each other before their engagement, he saw only a man whose heart had come to beat solely for the purpose of loving this woman. Perhaps his hesitancy to declare himself in love at the time stemmed more from fear of her not returning his affections; or perhaps he simply did not wish to rush, but there was no denying it: he had been hopelessly in love with Penelope Auckland since the moment they'd first met. And how she had made him happy in these short months.

There was one thing that he felt was missing, however; one thing that was needed to make his life utterly perfect. And that was a child, an heir to the dukedom. Odysseus knew that it would take time for them to conceive, but that knowledge didn't change the almost over-whelming desire to hold his own child in his arms, to raise them, teach them, guide them into adulthood. He cared not for the gender. He would love any life he and his wife conceived. But the absence of a baby was the one thing that cast a shadow over his otherwise perfect life.

He noticed Penelope looking at him with concern in her eyes from across the table. He smiled and shook his head, passing it off as him being distracted. He would not ruin the festivities. Not when Pene-lope had taken great care to throw such an extravagant event for the people of Ithaca. Besides, they had not even been married for three months, he told himself. It was too soon to think of babies. They were certainly trying as often as they could, and that was enough for now, he told himself. It had to be enough for now.

After dinner, more dancing commenced. Penelope had been asked to dance by another gentleman, so Odysseus stood and watched her, a smile on his face.

"You are most fortunate in your choice of a bride," said a voice to his left.

He turned and saw Baron Zachary Thunderstone standing next to him. The man's bright blue eyes flashed with understanding.

"She is sheer perfection, if you do not mind me saying so, Your Grace," the baron said.

Odysseus shook his head. "I do not mind at all, Thunderstone. Indeed, I have been meditating on that very truth and asking myself what it is I have ever done to deserve such favor from the gods."

Zachary nodded slowly. "Do you really think the gods had anything to do with it?"

Odysseus shrugged. "I do not know. It is a mystery just how much they are involved in our lives. And yet I feel so very fortunate in marrying Penelope that I cannot chalk it up to happenstance."

"Perhaps you underestimate your ability to make good choices?"

The duke laughed. "Perhaps. Although I really think it was she who chose me, not the other way around."

Zachary's eyes flashed and a smile lit his face. "Perhaps she was guided by Eros?" he said, casting a glance towards the duchess.

"Perhaps. Regardless of how it came to be, I thank the gods day and night for her."

"As well you should," Zachary said, looking back at Odysseus. "There is no knowing when that which we have been given will be taken away again."

Odysseus frowned at that. He turned and looked at the baron, his eyebrows furrowed. "Taken away? What do you mean, sir?"

Zachary shrugged, the light of the candles in the room catching brilliantly on his lightning-shaped pin. "Only that the gods decide our fate and it behooves us all to live each day in intentional appreciation for what we have, for we do not know if we will still have it the next morning."

"How very melodramatic of you," Odysseus said, trying not to be unnerved by the baron's words.

"I consider myself a realist, Your Grace. It is too easy to be caught up in one's blessings and happiness when tragedy is sure to strike all too soon. I do not mean to imply that we should never revel in our victories, but rather that we should revel with awareness. If that makes sense."

It did, although Odysseus did not like a word of it. He was put off, if he were being completely honest with himself, and did not know what to make of this warning the baron had given him. Odysseus was no stranger to tragedy. He had lived long enough in the world to know that horrible things happened often, and he had the emotional scars to prove the existence of his own grief and brokenheartedness. Yes, they should live as though they were not promised tomorrow, for of course they weren't. Odysseus had never seen the gods as particularly cruel, but there were occurrences in the world that they could stop and chose not to, and that Odysseus did not think he would ever understand.

His eyes flitted back to Penelope and a twinge of fear struck him. What number of ailments could befall her that might take her from him? How many ways were there that she could pass on suddenly and without warning? There were too many to count, and while he had known all of this before now, the truths had never really resonated in his heart. He felt himself growing afraid and tried to dismiss the feeling.

"Your Grace?"

Odysseus shook his head to clear his thoughts. "Yes, forgive me. I was lost in thought. What is it you were saying?"

"Simply that your wife is in excellent health, and she is a devoted, loyal, and faithful companion, and so you have no cause to fear for her," Zachary said, his penetrative gaze staring intently at Odysseus. "Unless, there is something you know that the rest of us do not about our new Duchess of Ithaca?"

Odysseus turned and faced the baron, his eyes flashing with anger and offense. "Are you questioning my wife's honor?"

The baron seemed surprised and shook his head head. "No, indeed, Your Grace. I only –"

Odysseus interrupted him, unwilling to listen to any explanation or excuse. "Forgive me, baron, but I am displeased with the turn this conversation has taken. Consider it a lapse in my own judgment, but you are posing questions that are out of turn, and I will not stand for them. Questioning my wife's honor to my face is not only ridiculous, but reckless. I think, perhaps, you should take your leave. Else I fear I will be quite unable to control myself."

Odysseus bowed and walked away, not even bothering to look over his shoulder to see if Baron Thunderstone had left. Inside, the fires of his anger were stoked again and again as he thought of everything the baron had said. How had the man gone from wishing Odysseus well to practically predicting Penelope's demise, and then landing finally on accusing her of infidelity, or something like it? Moreover, how had Odysseus not stopped him? Had it been any other man, Odysseus felt certain he would have thrown him out the moment he even hinted at something happening to Penelope, but the thought had not occurred to him.

So many questions ran through Odysseus's mind as he walked out of the ballroom towards the hall where wine and ale were served. He picked up a glass of red wine and sipped on it, unable to get the baron's words out of his head. What could have possibly possessed him to think such things appropriate conversation pieces for a ball? Or anywhere else, for that matter? It was astonishing, to say the least.

But what bothered Odysseus more than the baron's impertinences was his own reactions to them. Yes, he was angry and offended, but he was also frightened, unnaturally so. It felt as though Thunderstone's words had been premonitions, so heavily did they weigh on Odysseus's mind, and no matter how hard he tried to reassure himself that they meant nothing, he couldn't shake them. Every thought of their future was now laced with shadows of danger, whispers of heartache, and hints of secrecy. He knew there was nothing to them, that they were baseless and stemmed only from the ridiculous ramblings of a strange man with whom no one wanted anything to do, and yet deep down, Odysseus knew they were more than that. He could not accept them as prophecies, and so he called them possibilities, although the word didn't comfort him as he hoped it would.

And yes – of course they were possibilities. He could not see the future, so it was, indeed, possible that something bad would happen to Penelope. But there were also other possibilities filled with children and family and love. For every possibility of heartache, Odysseus thought of three more of bliss. He told himself to dismiss the baron's words and he did so.

Or, at least, he tried.

The dancing continued for another few hours. It was well into the dawn of the next day before everyone had left the manor and the ball was officially over. Odysseus and Penelope embraced, both of them thoroughly exhausted. But Odysseus did not immediately pull away from his wife. He held her close to him for a moment, just one extra moment, his eyes shut tight. She was here. She was with him, in his arms, alive and well. She was happy and healthy. She loved him. He loved her. All was well, he told himself.

"Odysseus?" she said, her voice breaking into his thoughts.

"Hmm?" he said, pulling back enough to look down into her face.

"Are you alright?"

He gave a smile and nodded. "Of course. Tonight was a profound success and I simply wanted to hold you and tell you how proud I am to have you at my side."

She smiled and kissed him. "I am quite exhausted. I shall retire, I think. Will you join me?"

He nodded. "Of course I will." He motioned for her to go first. "After you."

She turned and walked out of the ballroom and up the grand staircase towards their bed chamber. Odysseus followed. Yes, all was, indeed, well. He said this to himself with each step up the stairs. All was well. As well as it could possibly be.

It had to be well.

CHAPTER TWENTY

A Royal Letter

Mid-June, 13th Century B.C.E.

Foxcliff Manor,

Perichori, Ithaca,

Greece

A couple of weeks passed as Penelope and Odysseus continued to settle into their daily routine. Every morning they awoke and spent time in bed, their bodies tangled in the throws of passion. Then they would rise and dress in their respective rooms, make their way to the dining room where they breakfasted together, and then they parted, each of them with a list of the things they wanted to accomplish that day. Odysseus typically went to speak with Baxter about the estate and the very great need to hire a new apprentice. He had mentioned to the steward that they might consider hiring a woman to train under him but Baxter, ever the old-fashioned traditionalist, scoffed at the idea and refused outright. Odysseus had calmly reminded him that the choice was, in fact, his own, not Baxter's, and if Odysseus decided to hire a female apprentice, Baxter would be expected to treat her no differently than any other apprentice. Baxter's response had been a mere grunt and they had not returned to the subject since.

Penelope's days primarily consisted of going through Foxcliff Manor and making a list of improvements she wanted to implement. Changing wallpaper, removing and replacing old furniture, making sure the staff had everything they needed to complete their jobs efficiently, etc. She hadn't anticipated that such things would take as much time as they had, but often she would sit with the housekeeper and hours would pass by and she would only have gotten to a few items on her list. But it was important to her that the manor was kept up to date and in fashion, without spending too much money. Penelope, for all her love of stylish and modern things, was also frugal. She would not pursue an expensive purchase of anything without ensuring that it wouldn't jeopardize their ability to provide for everyone on their staff and cover any other necessary bills.

Twice each week, Odysseus would come home from working, bathe, dress in his black-tie, and then go to Pine's. Deverell Pine was known to be a particularly rambunctious man with seemingly insatiable appetites for good food and wine. Achilles and Patroclus, as well as others whom Odysseus considered friends, would be there and Penelope knew it made him happy to see them. But while she supported his recreational pursuits, she would have preferred that the club not bring in actresses and singers and other such women as often as it did. More than once each week she heard of some new scandal connected with Pine's; a gentleman had conceived a bastard with an actress one week, or a nobleman was seen consorting with a known adulteress the next. It wasn't that she feared Odysseus would be unfaithful, for that thought had never once crossed her mind. It was more that she didn't think it was becoming for a married man of any rank, but especially that of the upper echelons of Greek nobility, to frequent such an establishment.

She had mentioned it to Odysseus once in the first week after their honeymoon and he had passed it off as nothing of consequence.

"The men who get wrapped up in those scandals are doing a great deal more than meeting women at Pine's," he had said. "I know for a fact that the Marquess of Kioni has had mistresses a plenty for nearly a decade. Pine's was not the first club he frequented. His habit of infidelity was established a long time ago."

"But is it not scandalous simply to have women come into the club at all?" Penelope had asked.

Odysseus had shook his head. "I certainly do not think so. Most of the women are legitimate performers; actresses, singers, dancers, painters...they are there to entertain, not to seduce or entrap."

"And what of the few who are there to perform in other ways?"

He had sighed, clearly annoyed at her questions. And while he had offered her comfort and attempted to set her mind at ease, it hadn't worked. But she had let the matter drop, knowing that she did not want her husband to resent her simply because she disapproved of one of his favorite pastimes. Moreover, she felt she could trust both Achilles and Patroclus. Neither of them would be getting into any kind of nefarious trouble, and they would ensure Odysseus did not, either.

Penelope would have been lying, though, if she did not wonder about Odysseus's behaviors before they were engaged. As a bachelor, it would have been frowned on but acceptable for him to consort with another woman. Among the men who frequented Pine's, it would probably have been encouraged. She was not so naive as to believe that he had never felt the loving embrace of a woman before. And she could honestly say that she wasn't jealous or judgmental. What she couldn't honestly say was that did not care at all. But she kept her continually pressing concerns to herself, determined that she would not distrust her husband until she had reason to, and she truly believed that day would never come.

One evening in June as they sat and had luncheon together, a letter was delivered to Odysseus from King Menelaus. He opened the letter, read it, and then grinned.

"How would you fancy a trip to the mainland, my love?" he asked.

Penelope smiled. "I think that sounds lovely. Whatever for?"

"It is the King and Queen's anniversary in a few weeks, and we have been invited to the celebration."

"How wonderful! I have been meaning to write to the queen and invite her here, but every time I make a plan to do so, it escapes me. I shall be happy to be more acquainted with her." She took a sip of her tea and then set the cup back down. "How long would we be there?"

"Oh, at least a month," Odysseus said, taking a cucumber sandwich and putting the whole thing into his mouth. "Nothing Menelaus does is ever simple. He will want a great deal of feasting and revelry. There will, in all likelihood, be a tournament."

Penelope raised her eyebrows. "A tournament? I didn't realize they still jousted at the palace," she said sarcastically.

Odysseus laughed. "No, no. It'll be a tournament of other things: fencing, shooting, wrestling, and I'm sure there will be hunts nearly every day, along with balls and parties."

"It is sweet that he still celebrates his love for the queen so extravagantly after how long they have been married," Penelope said.

She meant it sincerely, but Odysseus laughed out loud. When he saw her confusion he stopped and raised his eyebrows.

"Are you in earnest?" he asked.

She nodded.

"Oh, darling, I am sorry. I thought you were jesting."

"Why would you think that?" she asked, genuinely confused.

"Well, it is common knowledge that there is no love between the king and queen. There never was. They kept up pretenses for as long as they could to give the kingdom hope for an heir and a peaceful future, but theirs was a marriage made for financial and social advantage. Nothing more."

"Oh," Penelope said, looking away for a moment. "Then, why the expense on such an extravagant celebration?"

"Because it is expected. It is the country's primary reprieve from this endless war with Troy. But the extravagance has nothing to do with his affection for the queen."

"That is very sad," she said, her mind reeling with thoughts as she recalled the king and queen's behavior at her and Odysseus's wedding.

Odysseus shrugged. "They knew what they were getting into," he said, finishing up his plate of sandwiches. "At any rate, we will be leaving in only a few days."

"So soon?" she asked, looking over at him.

"We cannot take our time when we receive an official summons from the king directly," he said. "We'd be leaving tomorrow if I didn't need to convince Baxter to bring on a female apprentice before we leave; I imagine it will take a lot of convincing, but the moment he has agreed to do so, we will make our way to the mainland."

"Well," she said, "I suppose I should get to packing."

She stood to leave, but Odysseus stood as well and took her hands in his. She looked up into his face and saw a great deal of love in his eyes, but also worry.

"How long until you know whether or not you are with child?" he asked.

She gave a soft smile. "Another week or so."

He nodded. "Can you...tell? Do you...think you know one way or the other how it will be?"

She shook her head. "I cannot predict if I am pregnant just by closing my eyes and asking my body, Odysseus."

He grinned. "Oh? I thought for sure the reincarnation of Hera herself, the goddess of fertility, would have had the power to do just that."

Penelope laughed. "You must not say such things!" she exclaimed. "The gods will not be mocked, my love."

"You know I don't believe in any of that," he said, pressing his lips to her neck and along her jawline and down her throat into her bosom.

"And you know that I most certainly do," she said, taking his face in her hands and lifting it to look into hers. "We will not be blessed with a child if you continue to discount the influence and power of the gods."

He pressed a kiss to the tip of her nose. "If you say so."

They shared an intimate kiss before parting ways. Odysseus went to meet with Baxter. Penelope went upstairs to organize her wardrobe and decide which gowns she would take with her to the mainland. And though her heart was happy and a smile lit her features, something in the back of her mind gnawed at her. It was gentle and easy enough to ignore, but there were moments when it persisted and broke into the forefront of her mind. She dismissed it as much as she could, and yet it still occupied her thoughts. It carried no specific question or idea or fear, and yet it was all three at once.

Something was not all that it seemed to be. She had felt it to be true since the night they had hosted the ball.

CHAPTER TWENTY-ONE

Reflections and Observations

Mid-June, 13th Century B.C.E.

Pine's Gentleman's Club

Vathi, Ithaca

Greece

The Pine's Gentleman's Club was located in the heart of Vathi. It was three stories tall, the building made entirely from brick. The inside was decorated in lavish couches, tables, chairs, as well as billiard tables, card tables for gambling, bars at which to sit and eat and drink, and more. It was almost always dimly lit, adding a mysterious and even seductive ambiance to the atmosphere. Gentlemen could smoke, drink, mingle, gamble, eat. The top floor was almost exclusively made of rooms with beds for when men were too drunk to take themselves home.

Pine's had existed in Ithaca for as long as anyone could remember. It had, presumably, passed from generation to generation, and yet few men ever claimed to have known the man who had run the establishment before Deverell Pine. Mr. Pine was a man of no noble or gentle standing. He had been born into a family of self-made men who had built Pine's into a fine and respected establishment that was prosperous and had been for some time. Deverell dressed in fine clothes and always made sure to sell only the best drink and food that Ithaca had to offer. He had a reputation to keep up and that meant never cutting corners on the quality of the services he offered.

Antinous sat at a table on the second floor eating a meal in silent reflection. It had been two months since Odysseus and Penelope had wed. Since then, he had worked tirelessly to improve his standing with Abigail and her father, and to much avail. His relationship with both of them had improved exponentially, and had come about through no meagerness of effort. He couldn't simply shower her with gifts, for that would have been seen as shallow. He had, instead, taken keen interests in the things which most fascinated her. They were mostly books and music, but he had exerted enormous effort in learning which books were her favorites so that he could read them and talk about them with her. He had learned she was especially fond of the new poet Sappho who had become renowned on the island of Lesbos and had purchased a signed copy for her.

Weeks and weeks of other such gestures had solidified his earnestness in wanting to make her happy, and he had, therefore, won back her respect and appeased her father's growing trepidations. He was now a welcome and expected guest at their home three times a week for dinner, and once a week he took an extra day to surprise her with a visit, flowers, and a trip into Vathi where he usually took her to dine followed by shopping at her favorite stores.

He hated every second of it, but knew he had to keep up appearances if his plan was going to work out in his favor. The young woman was sweet enough, he supposed, and her admiration of him did stroke his ego nicely, but he cared not for her outside of whatever it was he needed from her at any given moment. Although he had to admit, her father's recent elevation to the status of baron had been a pleasant and unexpected surprise for all of them. Baron Webb now earned an extra £300 every year from his title alone, and while it was not what Antinous would consider a significant amount of income, it did make his match with Abigail less embarrassing for himself.

He supposed he should consider himself lucky. There were some men and plenty of women who looked at him and Abigail enviously, and Antinous enjoyed that a great deal. He had also expected that she would be frivolous and extravagant in their shopping together, but she surprised him by never letting him buy her more than one item every time they went out. And usually, he had to prod her to let him buy that much. He had to admit that he admired that. It wasn't as if he couldn't afford to buy her everything nice and beautiful, and yet she seemed determined never to take him for granted.

Yes, there were many who would consider him lucky, indeed, but he could not go that far. For all her fine qualities, she bored him, and that made him despise her. There was a voice in the back of his mind that told him he was a worthless and undeserving fool for only pretending to like this girl. How much more would she worship him if he actually did give a damn about her? But that voice was quickly shushed and ignored. Antinous had no desire to be worshiped. Not by Abigail Webb, at any rate. No, there was only one woman whose adoration he desired, and she was currently unavailable to him.

For now, at least.

He smiled down at his plate of roasted pheasant, leafy greens with cucumbers and diced pears, and a white wine sauce that was positively decadent. He was proud of himself for concocting this plan regarding Odysseus and Penelope in the first place, let alone for how well it was going. It would take a great deal more time for his ultimate goals to come to fruition – years, in fact – but it would be worth it. He imagined the look he wanted to see on Odysseus's face and his smile widened even more. He could hardly wait, and yet he knew he would wait for as long as it took and he would do whatever it took to bring his plan about. He would have his moment. And Odysseus would be ruined.

A group of men came into the room at that moment, causing Antinous to look up from his food. He had hoped it was Baron Patterson Fish, one of the only men in Ithaca whom Antinous could stand, but he scowled when he saw it was only Odysseus with his entourage of friends. The two men locked eyes for a brief moment before Antinous, hating to even see the pompous duke's face, looked away and took a sip from his mug of ale. Odysseus, Achilles, Patroclus, and another officer in his majesty's army went to the bar and ordered drinks. They were deep in conversations regarding the ambiguous state of the war with Troy.

"I hear that there may soon be talks of peace," Patroclus said, taking his glass of red wine and leaning against the bar.

Achilles snorted. "I sure as hell hope not."

"Achilles, really," said Odysseus, taking his own glass of red wine and facing the other two gentlemen. "This war has taken a horrible toll on our citizens. You cannot possibly want it to continue?"

"In fact, I do," Achilles affirmed, ordering an ale.

"Why?" Patroclus asked. "When you know the consequences have already been dire?"

Achilles shrugged. "I do not like Troy. Their king, Priam, is an old man with nothing better to do than stir up trouble. His soldiers are weak and I hope that we will destroy them utterly."

"You do realize we are losing the war?" Odysseus asked. "We have been losing the war since it started."

Again, Achilles shrugged. "Of course we are. King Menelaus won't commit to a full scale invasion, neither did his father, and nothing less than that will ensure our victory."

"You make it sound like you disapprove of the king's choice?" Patroclus asked.

"I do disapprove. A courageous man would do what was needed to defeat Troy and thereby end the war."

"Did you just call your king, your commander, a coward?" Odysseus asked, standing up straight.

He looked prepared to fight Achilles if the man did not respond approvingly. Antinous shook his head to himself. Odysseus was willing to fight his best friend over words he did not want to hear coming out of the fighter's mouth. Words that Antinous would have bet £100 Odysseus agreed with. He had to give it to him: at least the duke was consistent.

"What would you call him?" Achilles asked, seemingly uncon-cerned with Odysseus's body language.

"I would call him my king," Odysseus said forcefully, "and I would do well to remember that, whatever my personal opinions, it is treason to speak against him."

"Then what would you say of his choices?" Achilles demanded. "How he continues to send as few fighters as possible to the front lines when he knows that doing so will only prolong what has become a stagnant and expensive war with a foreign territory?"

"I'd say he is hesitant to put lives in danger needlessly," Odysseus responded. "And that he cares more about saving the lives of his sol-diers than he does conquering a country in a war that he did not start." The duke's eyes stared hard into his friend's. "And I would say that such a choice takes a profound sense of selflessness as well as courage, knowing that he will face criticism, while still doing what he believes is right."

Achilles stared at him for a moment, then lifted his glass in a sar-castic salute (whether to Odysseus or the king, Antinous wasn't sure), downed the wine, and left the room in a huff. Patroclus called after him, but the man didn't slow or turn. He slammed the door behind him. Antinous had to force himself to stifle his laughter. Now was not the time to antagonize Odysseus, but he found it endlessly amusing that the man thought so highly of himself, he had offended his best friend in the entire world, and had done so without any hesitation. Was the duke capable of keeping any of his loved ones happy?

"All the better for me," Antinous muttered under his breath.

A moment later, Deverell Pine walked into the room and smiled brightly. "Your Grace!" he exclaimed. "I was told you had arrived. Welcome back!"

Odysseus bowed and shook hands with Deverell. "Thank you, Pine. It is great to be here. Although it will be some weeks before I return, and I thought I should settle my tab before I left for the mainland."

Deverell's eyebrows arched in surprise. "To the mainland, eh? Whatever for?"

"The duchess and I have been invited to celebrate the anniversary of the king and queen," Odysseus replied. "And we all know the king loves his celebrations."

Deverell laughed and nodded. "Yes, indeed he does. Well, we will miss you here, Halstead," he said, dropping the formalities. "But you will be welcome back at any time. Do, please, remember that."

Odysseus nodded and pulled out several pounds and placed them on the bar. Deverell took the money, counted it, and gave the duke back 20 pence. Patroclus shook his head.

"Do you really have every account memorized, Pine?" he asked.

"Indeed I do, Lieutenant," he said with a grin. "I keep an extremely accurate set of books with every single transaction that I have managed since I took over this place. I don't know if it's the attention I take when going over my finances or if I've been blessed by the gods, but every single number stays right here," he said, tapping on his left temple.

Just then, the door opened and four women entered. Three of them looked as though they had just come from performing a concert or a play, and one of them was as scantily dressed as she could be without too obviously revealing her profession. Antinous smiled. He had come here for distraction and, while he refused to let himself succumb physically (Pine's was too public a place to let himself express his more carnal desires), this would ease his mind of the things that weighed on him. But he did notice that upon the women's arrival, Odysseus downed his glass of wine, thanked Deverell for the excellent service, and then quickly left.

It was not the first time Antinous had witnessed this. Odysseus would play billiards and he would gamble and drink and smoke to his heart's content, but the moment that women were brought into the club, he left. He neither looked at nor spoke to any of the women. He clearly intended to keep his reputation clean of even the whisper of scandal.

Antinous remembered, then, what Sir Hawthorn Satchel had said some months before, about how there were rumors that Penelope had trapped the duke into marriage. Antinous had dismissed the claim some weeks later when it became clear that the duchess was not with child and their wedding had not, therefore, been an attempt to repair or save her reputation. But now it did occur to him that even if the duchess was not pregnant, it did not necessarily follow that the rumors were untrue. She could have still seduced him and, even without a pregnancy, manipulated him into marrying her to save her reputation.

Would a man so determined to avoid even the hint of scandal allow himself to be seduced? Antinous found himself thinking over every interaction he had witnessed between Odysseus and any woman to try and find something, anything, that he might use against the duke, but nothing came to mind. If Penelope had seduced Odysseus, there would never be any way to prove it. And it would be difficult, indeed, to manufacture a situation in which the duke found himself in a compromising situation if he wouldn't even look at other women now that he was married.

But of course, Antinous reminded himself, the duke was still in the first months of marriage. The throws of love and marital bliss were strong, but they would not last forever. Odysseus was a man of principle and clearly expected everyone in his life to rise to his standard of propriety. It was only a matter of time before cracks would form between Odysseus and Penelope, and through them, the seeds of strife would be sown. Antinous smiled widely to himself at the thought. Yes, this was going to be worth the wait.

CHAPTER TWENTY-TWO

To the Mainland

In only a few days Penelope and Odysseus were on their way to mainland Greece. They traveled the first day from their estate in Perichori to the port of Ag Andrea in southern Ithaca. They spent the night in a fancy hotel and then sailed out of the harbor the next morning. It was nearly summer now and the weather was fine, albeit a bit windy for Penelope's preference. Still, she had never before sailed on a ship and the experience of being out on the open ocean was one she thoroughly enjoyed.

They hadn't eaten that morning, so once the ship set sail, they made their way below deck to the first class dining room. Odysseus asked for, and was granted, a table next to one of the only windows in the room. This made Penelope exceedingly happy. She couldn't see much of either what was above the water or beneath it, but even just seeing the waves splash against the ship's hull was enough to excite her.

They ordered a simple breakfast of muffins with butter, honey, and jam, hot black tea with cream, and a light but refreshing fruit salad that Penelope was especially fond of.

"Do you think the celebrations will go well?" Penelope asked as they ate.

Odysseus shrugged. "There's no telling. Last year, they hardly spoke to one another the entire two weeks of parties and balls and tournaments. And though the king was clearly amused by everything around him, he made no effort to hide the fact that he most certainly was not celebrating his marriage to the queen."

Penelope furrowed her eyebrows. "Not even for the sake of appearances? Surely it is better for his people if they believe the king and queen to at least be friends, if not lovers?"

"Neither of them wanted the marriage," Odysseus said, taking a sip of his tea. "Menelaus' father was the one who arranged it and he practically had to pay Helen's entire dowry himself to convince her father to agree. The women who marry into the Wylde royal house typically do not live long, and Helen's father did not want to watch his only child waste away in the shadow of another Wylde king. He only agreed to grant his permission after Menelaus' father told him to keep Helen's dowry."

Penelope's eyes widened. "So he sold his daughter to the Wylde family?"

Odysseus nodded. "That he did."

"Why? Were there not other women who would have gladly become queen?"

Odysseus smiled. "A marriage to the heir of the royal throne is one that must come with benefits to the royal house. The late king may not have gotten Helen's dowry, but he did get an entire army of soldiers and seamen in exchange. That was a prize no other eligible woman could offer."

"Were they not already his late majesty's soldiers and seamen?"

He shook his head. "No, they were mercenaries that Helen's father had employed for nearly a decade. They were not Greek citizens and could not, therefore, be conscripted into the army or the navy against their will. Once the marriage between Helen and Menelaus was consummated, those mercenaries no longer served Helen's father. They served her father-in-law."

"How many of these mercenaries were there?"

"Above ten thousand."

Penelope's eyes widened. "Ten thousand? And what has become of them all in that time?"

"Most are still living, though they have been occupying the shores outside of Troy for over a decade now."

"And their majesties could not find even one thing between them that might lead to friendship or mutual respect? Even within a marriage neither of them wanted?"

"I was not there for every moment of their marriage, my darling, so I can only repeat what I have heard from the king himself. He said they tried. He said they failed. I did not ask clarifying questions."

"Then, why celebrate a marriage they both wish they could undo? Why not undo it, for that matter, now that his father is dead?"

"Because the kingdom needs their king to be married. The kingdom needs an heir."

"They aren't trying to have a baby, are they?"

Odysseus shook his head. "I don't think they ever have."

"Then it is all for appearances? Even the reason they stay together is a pretense for the sake of their subjects only? As some kind of beacon of hope for something that will never happen?"

"It is a tragic reality, but yes."

Penelope was quiet. She did not understand it. Surely a festive celebration like the one they were attending would only call more attention to the fact that the king and queen did not love each other? She supposed only the king and queen's most intimate friends would know the truth of it. And the absence of a celebration would certainly plant seeds of doubt in the minds of those not already privy to the truth.

She realized it wasn't the logistics she didn't understand, but the reality itself. The king said the two of them had tried to make their marriage happy, and so she should believe they had, but she found herself unable to. How could the king not at least admire and respect his wife? And how could she not at least feel the same for her husband? They did not need to love each other, but surely there were enough good qualities between them to make mutual respect a possibility? Or perhaps there was some information no one knew that prohibited this? She didn't know why it bothered her so much, but the thought did weigh heavily on her for the rest of their meal.

Once they had finished their breakfast, she and Odysseus walked out onto the deck and stood at the railing. They could see nothing but the ocean for miles in any direction and Penelope loved every moment. The smell of the air, heavily salted due to the rush of wind over the surface of the waves, was intoxicating. It surprised her how much stronger the ocean scent was when they were on the water as opposed to when they were on shore, but it was a surprise she enjoyed.

As they stood and watched the waves roll by, Penelope let out a deep sigh. She was happy. Profoundly happy and content with her life and what it was shaping into. She had a husband who was clever as well as kind, gentle as well as handsome, and generous as well as rich. She lived a vastly comfortable life and was lucky enough to boast of a happy marriage based on mutual love and respect. She couldn't imagine anything that might make her more happy than she already was, aside from granting Odysseus his one remaining heart's desire and giving birth to a child. But that would come in time, she told herself.

"We have a room below deck," Odysseus said, leaning in close to her. "Complete with a bed, in case you...wanted to rest a while."

Penelope grinned and looked up at her husband. "Would this...resting...come complete with your tongue between my legs, perhaps?"

His eyes flashed with carnal hunger and the corners of his lips turned up into a seductive grin. "Only unless you tell me you don't want it," he said, his voice low.

"Then I think that yes, Your Grace, I do fancy a rest just now."

They walked arm-in-arm down into the hull of the large ship and Odysseus led her to the bedroom. Or, rather, the cabin, for it certainly was not large enough to be called a room. But for its small size, it still boasted a bed and a desk near the window. Odysseus shut the door behind them and locked it.

"How long until we reach port?" Penelope asked, already undoing the laces of her day dress.

"At least another eight hours or so," Odysseus said. "Longer, if we encounter harsh weather."

"Eight hours should be enough," she said, letting her dress fall to the floor.

Moments later, they were naked, standing before each other. They had both long moved past the awkwardness of seeing each other naked and now, Penelope was glad to find that she genuinely loved the sight of her husband's body. He was a tall man and largely built with muscles that were well defined. He was strong, which only made her all the more wild with passion when they made love because he was always, without fail, so very tender. And gentle. He could have been rough, he could have been forceful, and yet he always took great care to ensure not only her comfort, but her pleasure. She did not think he would ever have enjoyed her body if he did not know beyond a shadow of any doubt that she wanted him as much as he wanted her.

"I...have a request this time," she said, feeling herself blush as he stepped over to her and pressed his lips against her forehead.

"Yes?" he asked, pressing a kiss to her cheek, and then another to her jawline, and then another to her neck.

"I..." she laughed breathlessly as his hands wrapped around her, though his lips stayed at her neck. "I don't know if I can say..."

"I cannot please you if you do not tell me what to do, Pen," he said, using the nickname that she had come to adore.

"You won't judge me?"

His chuckle ticked the skin of her throat as his lips moved around her neck from side to the other. "You have my solemn vow."

"I want you to fuck me."

He froze and moved backward quickly, his eyes wide. She didn't know if he was surprised or angry, and then he smiled widely and raised his eyebrows. "I did not know you were even familiar with that word."

She blushed fiercely, but didn't look away or stop smiling. She would not reveal how she had learned it unless he explicitly asked because the embarrassment she felt would kill her, for sure. He picked her up and laid her onto the bed, holding himself above her by propping himself up on his elbows.

"Are you certain?" he asked.

Penelope nodded. "Yes," she said, trying not to sound as though she was whining or begging, but she was eager for him to be inside of her. And it wasn't as though he hadn't been somewhat rough before, but he always seemed to be so in control, so completely aware of how everything he did affected her. She loved it, she truly did, but she wanted to know more than just the tenderness of making love. She wanted to know the fullness of his carnal desires.

He smiled down at her and pressed a kiss to her forehead. "Another time I'll make you beg for it," he said, sliding inside of her.

She was already wet and aroused. They kissed and wrapped their arms around one another as he moved, but even though she thoroughly enjoyed being one with him, she couldn't say she felt as though his movements were any different than they usually were. She was about to break their kiss and say something when she realized he was moving her right leg up to her side, bending it at the knee. She furrowed her eyebrows a bit and then felt how deep he went into her on his next thrust and let out an involuntary moan of pleasure. He had never been so deep inside of her before and the sensation was unlike any she had ever felt.

"Try not to be too loud," he said, "We want to still look the other passengers and crew in the eye when we leave this room."

She smiled and nodded, and the fucking began. He was not really rough, not at first. He slid into her as deeply as he could with each thrust, but his movements were slow. She didn't quite understand how this was the fucking she had read about until the pressure began to build deep inside of her. It was as though his body, his erection, was plucking at something hidden inside of her, heightening her arousal.

"Does it hurt?" he asked.

She shook her head. "No, it feels good."

He smiled and began to move her other leg, widening them to better accommodate his hips and thighs. She adjusted herself, too, and suddenly he was as deep as he could go and her vision blurred. Her head swam as overwhelming lust filled her body. She gasped and moaned and groaned with each movement of his hips, the pressure continuing to build. She couldn't climax without his fingers between her legs, though, surely? She never had before, but then he had also never shoved himself this deeply inside of her.

His movements quickened. He still thrusted himself just as deep and just as hard, but his movements were faster. She looked up into his face and saw him staring down at her with love, but also a ferocity that made her stomach fill with flutters. It made her throb and ache, seeing that look in his eyes.

"Do not hold back," she whispered, hoping that she wouldn't regret the words.

Odysseus pulled out of her, turned her around until she was on fours, and then slid back inside of her again. It was a completely different sensation now and she let out another moan as the pressure inside of her turned to pleasure. Yes, she was going to climax. The build was slow, despite how quickly and how hard Odysseus was thrusting. She had been propped up on her hands, but now she bent down onto her elbows and the pleasure was only further heightened still.

"Odysseus," she said as the pleasure built into ecstasy, but still the climax did not come. "Do not...stop."

She heard Odysseus grunt and closed her eyes, focusing on the immense and multifaceted pleasure she felt with each movement. She wanted to touch herself, but she also didn't want to ruin whatever was happening inside of her. Whatever this kind of climax was, she wanted to experience it in full.

And she did. A moment later, the release came hot and hard and she buried her face in the pillows, unable to keep herself from screaming. Odysseus let out a moan and cursed, but he didn't slow or stop, and even as her first climax receded, another crashed over her and she screamed again.

"Was that...two in a row?" Odysseus asked.

She couldn't speak, so she turned her head towards him and nodded.

"Well, let's see how many we can count, shall we?"

Penelope was a mess and couldn't answer. She just nodded and he began again in earnest. The third climax, like the first, took time to build and then crashed over her in another hard rush of sensations and pleasure. Only this one didn't recede. The same pleasure, the same rush and heat and pressure, fell over her again without fading and then started building from that climax into an even greater one. It was as though every movement, every thrust of his hips was enough to make each release beget another. She stopped counting, too overwhelmed by pleasure to think of anything else.

Before she knew what was happening, she was on her back again and Odysseus was staring down into her eyes.

"I love you," he said.

"I love you, too," she replied, certain that her words were slurred together.

He slid inside of her and quickly returned to the intensity of fucking. Penelope could feel the place within her, that deep spot calling out for him. She began to move her own hips, desperate to feel him pluck at that place like a string, desperate for another release. She moaned as it began to work, surprised that she could find release in so many different ways.

"You drive me wild, Penelope," he said.

"Can you...can you fuck me any harder?" she asked.

"Are you sure?" he asked with a grin. "I haven't exactly been gentle with you."

She moaned and writhed beneath him. "I just...I need you deeper."

He propped himself up on his hands, one to either side of her. She bent her knees and spread her legs wide for him. And then he was back to thrusting as hard and as deep as he could, eliciting moans of pleasure from Penelope. She could have cried for how good he felt.

"Please," Odysseus said, "let me watch you climax."

She nearly slid her hand between her legs to bring the release faster, but she decided she liked the build up, the agony and bliss of wanting the release, of being ever so close, but not quite there. Odysseus groaned loudly. She was growing tighter around him. She could feel it herself. She wondered if she could tease him by clenching those muscles. She tried. He practically shouted with pleasure.

"Did you do that on purpose?" he asked.

She smiled, biting her bottom lip. "Maybe."

"Will you do it again?" he asked.

She did. The pleasure it brought to her was only increased when she saw that it was enough to almost make him climax. They stared into each other's eyes and Penelope knew another release was building. She moaned, her breathing quickening.

"Don't hold back," he whispered, repeating the words she had spoken to him when they first began.

She cried out in pleasure as the climax washed over her. He let out several loud groans and grunts as he reached his own climax, and then he rolled onto his back, breathing heavily. Her vision was blurry and the room was spinning as though she had drank too much wine, but when she thought of how she felt, a wide smile lit her face. She felt better than she had ever felt. She tingled everywhere. She was still throbbing in the aftermath of ecstacy.

"I...didn't even...touch myself..." she whispered, looking over at him.

Odysseus smiled. "Sometimes you do not have to. Though I do not understand the why of it."

Penelope laughed breathlessly. "Do you...know how many..."

Odysseus chuckled. "I lost count at six."

They giggled together and Odysseus moved over and wrapped his arms around her. Her skin tingled even more as his body came in contact with hers again, even though there was nothing sexual in his embrace.

"I think I really do need a nap now," she said.

He nodded, already half asleep. "As do I."

She thought that it would be prudent that they at least put some clothes on before allowing themselves to slumber, but she didn't move and in the next moment, consciousness left her. The last thought she remembered before falling asleep was how much she loved being in her husband's arms.

CHAPTER TWENTY-THREE

Royal Contention

It took them several more hours to sail from Ag Andrea to Lepreum, the harbor on the mainland in which their ship made port. Both Penelope and Odysseus spent the rest of their sail in the dining cabin and on the deck. The weather remained very fine and it made passage easy. They had luncheon around noon and then a few hours after that, the ship made port. Neither Odysseus nor Penelope felt like starting their journey by carriage so soon after disembarking the ship, and so they took a room at an inn on the coast. It was not a large room, but it met their needs for the evening. They dined at the restaurant attached to the inn and then retired early. They were exhausted from traveling all day and were in great need of sleep.

The next morning they awoke at dawn, breakfasted at the restaurant, and then hired a carriage to take them into Sparta. They would be traveling nearly eighty miles over the course of two days and they intended to make as good a time as possible. There was no way they would make it in a single day, no matter how desirous they were to do so, and so they opted for a more comfortable journey. The first day they did, indeed, make it nearly fifty miles, stopping only to take their luncheon at noon and then again to rest for the night at an inn an hour or so outside of Thuria. They ate a large dinner and retired for the evening and awoke again at dawn to complete the last trek of their journey across mainland Greece. They spent most of the day traveling and arrived in Sparta before sunset.

They were greeted by both King Menelaus and Queen Helen at the entrance to the palace.

"Odysseus!" Menelaus said, throwing his arms out wide and embracing his lifelong friend. "It is good to see you! We were hoping you'd arrive yesterday, but you had to take your time, I see."

"We would have preferred to arrive yesterday as well, sire, but alas, the journey required two full days, it seems," Odysseus replied.

Helen and Penelope curtsied to one another and Helen offered the young woman a friendly smile.

"I am glad there will be another woman here with me," the queen said, taking Penelope's hands in her own. "I am surrounded by nothing but men just now and I feel I shall go mad if I do not have a woman's company soon."

"I am honored to be that woman, Your Highness," Penelope replied. "Indeed, I think I could use the companionship of my own sex, too. I have not seen any of my own friends for some weeks."

"Well, that is not surprising," Helen said with a mischievous smile, "considering how recently the two of you were married. I would be surprised if you saw anyone at all other than your husband. It would mean you are spending entirely too much time out of bed."

Penelope blushed and laughed, caught off guard by the queen's pointed sense of humor.

"Are you hungry?" Helen asked. "Do you need refreshment after your journey?"

Penelope looked over at Odysseus and then said, "I think some time to refresh ourselves would be wonderful, though I do not wish to postpone your supper."

Helen shook her head. "No, no, we already ordered supper to be served late so that you could join us. You will be shown to your chamber to rest and change, and then we will convene in the dining hall in two hours for the evening meal. Does that sound alright?"

Penelope smiled and nodded. "Yes, Your Highness. That sounds wonderful."

The four of them split up and Odysseus and Penelope were shown to their room. They were given warm baths and then they took a brief nap, asking the servants to wake them in thirty minutes or so. Then they changed into nicer attire for supper and made their way through the palace to meet the king and queen. As Penelope and Odysseus neared the dining hall, they heard the royal couple speaking in raised voices. The two of them slowed for a moment, not wishing to interrupt their conversation.

"The country cannot continue like this," Helen said, her voice filled with desperation and anger. "We have lost too many of our men to this war and the country is facing economic collapse."

"It is bad enough that my advisors do not support me in my decisions on this matter, but must I now be pestered by my own wife?" Menelaus asked, his voice low but filled with bitterness.

"This is more important than your pride, Menelaus! Kings have been overthrown by their subjects for less than what you and your father have done to your own people. If you are not careful, if you do not measure your next steps with intention, you may find yourself on the wrong end of a pitchfork."

"Are you threatening me, woman?" Menelaus shouted, his voice echoing off the walls of the hallway. "Because that is treason, and do not think I won't throw you in a dungeon for it!"

"I've been living in worse than a dungeon since your father bought me from mine and gave me to you," Helen said, her voice thick with bitterness.

Menelaus laughed. "You think this place is worse than a dungeon? And your clothes, all made of the finest fabrics; I suppose you fancy them your rags? Though selling them would feed almost every family in this city for a month or more? And what of your jewels? Are they chains that force you to stay here against your will?" The sarcasm in his voice was heavy.

"A gilded cage is still a cage and marriage to a king I did not choose is still imprisonment, yes," she exclaimed. "I have done my utmost to be as good a wife to you as I am able. I have never once begrudged your many infidelities, though the gods know I have never been given the same opportunity to pursue my own happiness, fleeting as it might be. I have given you the best years of my life and now the only other solace afforded to me is long past possibility! Motherhood was the one reprieve I clung to. Now, I am too old to bear any children, and still you can barely stand my being in the same room as you!"

Penelope and Odysseus shared a look. They both knew they should walk away, and yet neither of them moved to do so.

"You talk to me of honor and duty and yet you have always made it your business to doubt me, question me, supplant me!"

"Supplant you?" Helen shouted. "When have I ever –"

"Do not pretend at ignorance!" Menelaus roared. "I saw the letter myself! You wrote to your brother less than six years ago and begged that he 'do what he could to remove his royal family from the palace in Sparta'," he said, glaring at his wife, "You said it was the one thing that would give you peace. And you deny that this was a conspiracy to remove me from my throne?"

Helen laughed loudly. "Your grasp on reality is truly tenuous if you read that letter and thought I was referring to you."

"If not I, then whom?"

"Me!" Helen screamed, her voice lifting into a high-pitched screech. "I was begging him to come here and remove me from this place, to take me home where I could live out the remainder of my lonely, miserable life in some kind of peace!"

Menelaus did not immediately respond. Odysseus, curious to see what was happening, leaned over enough to peer into the dining hall. He saw the king and queen standing within only a few feet of each other.

"You...you really weren't trying to have me removed from the throne?" asked Menelaus, his voice calmer now.

"Why would I want you removed from the throne?" Helen asked.

He shrugged. "The throne is power. Doesn't everyone want power?"

Tears were on Helen's cheeks. She shook her head. "You really have never known me at all, have you?" She let out a sad chuckle. "I never wanted the throne, Menelaus. I never wanted power. I didn't even want this marriage, but once we were wed, the only thing I wanted was for us to make the most out of this life we were thrust into. Instead, I have been given only your resentment, your anger, and your apathy."

"I..." the king seemed lost for words. "I really thought you were trying to take the throne..."

"Then why didn't you have me imprisoned?"

He shrugged again. "Your brother is a powerful man with an enormous army of his own. If he had decided to attack, I would have lost the battle and the throne would have been taken from me anyway."

She nodded slowly. "So the throne is really the only thing you've ever loved?"

Penelope took Odysseus's hand and tugged on it. They had stayed too long and it was time they went back to their room. He turned to follow her but in doing so, must have made some sound because Menelaus called out, "Is that you, Odysseus?"

Odysseus and Penelope shared an awkward glance and then turned to walk back towards the dining hall. They both knew to pretend that they had heard nothing. They walked into the dining hall and Odysseus smiled widely.

"Yes, my king," he said, bowing. "I apologize for the delay. We took a nap and ended up sleeping longer than we had intended."

Menelaus waved his hand. "No apologies, no apologies. Please, sit. We're just happy you were able to make it."

"Has no one else arrived yet?" Penelope asked.

"Agamemnon and Clytemnestra will be here tomorrow," Menelaus said, casting a glance at Helen who kept her head down. "I believe everyone else has taken lodgings in the city."

"I understand there will be a ball in a fortnight," Penelope said, smiling sweetly. "I am looking forward to that very much."

"I'm sure your husband feels much the same," Menelaus said with a smile and a wink at Odysseus.

"Oh, I know very well how he despises dancing," Penelope said, "but he has agreed to dance with me several times throughout the evening, as he knows how much I love it."

Odysseus smiled at her. "I could never deprive you of something you love when it requires so little from me to make you so happy."

Penelope smiled sincerely, her heart fluttering in her chest. She saw both Menelaus and Helen blanch at them, but pretended she hadn't noticed. It was probably difficult for them to see a happily married couple before them when their own marriage was so tumultuous. Indeed, Penelope made a mental note that she would keep anymore effusions of love and affection to herself while in Sparta.

"And I shall see to it that he keeps it," Menelaus said, casting a stern look at Odysseus, "for no friend of mine would ever rescind on such a promise."

"I assure you, my king, I have no intention to rescind," Odysseus said, taking a sip of his wine as the servants filled his glass.

"How long is the tournament going to be, Your Majesty?" Penelope asked, feeling as though the subject should be changed.

"Two months," Menelaus said as a delicious, creamy soup was brought out for the first course. "It begins tomorrow and will last through the end of August."

"I've never attended a tournament before," Penelope said, taking a bite of her soup. "I am excited to see what one entails."

"It's mostly a lot of very drunk men who think they're much better at fighting than they actually are who, after more drinking, make utter asses out of themselves," Helen said, looking over at Menelaus with a smile. "Isn't that right, darling?"

Menelaus glared at her for a moment and then shrugged. "It's not a celebration if you're not drinking to excess," he said, looking over at Odysseus.

Penelope watched as Odysseus smiled and lifted his glass towards the king. He seemed content and pleased to be back with his oldest friend, but Penelope could tell he was uncomfortable and perhaps even angry. She had only seen him angry on the very rarest of circumstances and he was skilled at keeping his darker emotions hidden, so she couldn't be sure how displeased he was with the king. But there was enough of a cloud in his eyes to convince her that he was, at least, upset.

"Did you enjoy your honeymoon?" Helen asked.

Penelope smiled and nodded. "We did, indeed. A few close friends visited us a couple of times during those three weeks, but otherwise it was just us two."

"As it should be," Menelaus said with a grin. "I assume there will be a future duke or duchess of Ithaca on the way soon?" he added.

Penelope did not know how to answer, but luckily Odysseus interjected.

"Our lives have been a bit too hectic of late to really think earnestly of children," he said. "We are anxious to start a family, of course, but only when the time is right."

Penelope felt his answer was somewhat rehearsed and hollow. And even dishonest. They had not only been thinking of children, they had been actively attempting to conceive almost from their wedding night. Why had he lied to the king? Had something changed that she did not know?

"Well that's certainly a smart choice," Menelaus said. "But I will feel better when we know that the Halstead line is secure."

"I doubt that the duke and duchess take your preferences into account when it comes to starting their own family, my love," Helen said coldly.

No one missed the glare that Menelaus cast towards Helen. Penelope found herself wishing that they had left the hallway the moment they realized the king and queen were fighting. Penelope wracked her brain to think of anything to say, some point of conversation that would distract from the awkwardness brewing between them all. She could think of nothing. She did not know either of them well enough to appeal to their respective interests, and given what she had overheard only moments before, Penelope was not inclined to make things easier for the king. In fact, she rather believed he deserved to be as awkward and uncomfortable as possible, but Helen certainly did not. Yet she could think of nothing to say that would appeal to her interests, either.

She wondered if, perhaps, it would be best for her and the queen to leave the dining hall, then? Yes, she decided, that was the best choice. She set down her spoon and placed her napkin on the table.

"Forgive me," she said, "but I'm feeling a bit warm. I think I could use a walk in the gardens, if that is alright?"

She saw Odysseus give her a slight nod of approval and felt relieved that yes, this was, indeed, the right course of action.

"I'd be happy to join you," Helen said, standing to her feet. "Unless you'd rather be alone?"

"No, Your Highness. I would be most grateful for your company."

The men stood as two women curtsied and then Helen and Penelope made their way out of the dining hall.

Chapter Twenty-Four

A Duke and The King

Once the two women had left, Odysseus asked Menelaus if they could move into the study and talk over cigars and brandy. Odysseus wanted to leave the emotionally charged setting of the dining hall. If he was going to talk frankly with Menelaus, he wanted to ensure that none of the servants would interrupt, either. The king readily agreed and they made their way into the study. It was a large room filled with busts of Menelaus' family members and hunting trophies mounted on the walls. Odysseus waited until he and Menelaus had settled into their chairs with cigars and brandy before he initiated conversation. He knew this would not be pleasant, but it was one he felt obligated to have.

"I feel I should be honest," Odysseus said, "about what Penelope and I overhead before dinner between yourself and the queen."

Menelaus looked up from his brandy, his eyes dark and filled with sadness and frustration.

"I wondered how much you had heard," he muttered.

"The two of you were quite loud, Your Majesty," Odysseus said.

Menelaus sighed. "Well, let me have it. Tell me how bad a mess I am making of my marriage."

Odysseus shrugged. "Sounds to me like you already know that."

Menelaus leaned forward with his elbows on his knees. "I have tried, Odysseus. I have tried as hard as I can to make my marriage into something I can tolerate, but it is impossible."

"What about what Helen can tolerate?"

Menelaus frowned and looked up at him. "What?"

"You said you've tried making your marriage into something you can tolerate, but you say nothing of your wife or her happiness."

"And?"

Odysseus guffawed and shook his head. "Come, Your Majesty, you know what I am saying. If you are only focused on your own comfort but not your wife's, then of course your endeavors are going to fail. Marriage is not meant to benefit only one party."

Menelaus rolled his eyes. "That is easy for you to say when you are married to that beautiful creature."

Odysseus felt his heart swell with pride and disappointment simultaneously. "I do not deny that it brings me joy to hear my wife praised so by Your Majesty, but it disheartens me to hear you so obviously slight your own wife who is, by all accounts, one of the most beautiful and desirable women in the world." When Menelaus did not respond, Odysseus continued. "There are a great many people throughout Greece and beyond who would consider themselves fortunate, indeed, to simply be graced with a smile from the queen. And yet you can barely stand to be around her, and make no secret of the fact."

"Like I said, I have tried, and to no avail." Menelaus downed his brandy and poured himself another glass.

"You are not the only one who was forced into a marriage you did not want," Odysseus said. "And can you really say that you have done everything you can to be a good husband to Helen?"

Menelaus turned angry eyes on Odysseus. "Are you questioning my dedication as a husband?"

"Yes," Odysseus said without hesitation, "and harshly. You make no secret of your many affairs with multiple women. I do not doubt that you have plenty of illegitimate children as well. Meanwhile, your wife lives out her days alone, without solace, knowing her husband despises her, even though she has done nothing to deserve it."

Menelaus scoffed. "Hasn't she?" He shook his head. "She has never supported me, even in the face of ridicule from my advisors and war council. She only criticizes me. Nothing else."

"Because you give her only things to criticize," Odysseus stated, knowing he was treading on dangerous ground, and unwilling to pull back. "How is she to support you when you do not listen to anyone?"

Menelaus downed his second glass of brandy and poured a third. "She does not even try," he said, setting down his cigar. "And I know my advisors use her to needle me with their desires for peace, and she has become a willing pawn in their game."

"They go to her because you refuse to hear reason," Odysseus said, his voice filled with frustration.

"She has betrayed me," Menelaus stated. "Even in the early years of our marriage, she pushed herself into matters that were not her concern."

"She is the queen, Menelaus. Anything relating to the safety of Greece is her concern, just as it is yours."

"But I am the king!" Menelaus shouted. "My word is the highest authority, granted by the divine right of the gods. She should ultimately stand at my side and support me, and yet she has never done so. Not once." He ran a hand over his face in frustration. "I have never claimed to be a perfect man, Odysseus. But even with my failings, I have tried to do right by those depending on me. She cannot even acknowledge that much!"

"I believe that you are trying to do right by your citizens, but I will not agree that you have ever done right by your wife," Odysseus said, staring into his friend's eyes.

"She is not the part she pretends to play in company," the king muttered.

"And this is deserving of your infidelities and cruel neglect?" Odysseus asked, raising his eyebrows. He was thoroughly disappointed in and disgusted by his king's attitude and behaviors.

"You are not the king!" Menelaus shouted. "You do not know of what you speak!"

"I believe I do. I am not a king, but I have a dukedom and subjects who look to me for guidance and leadership. My choices greatly impact the people depending on me. I have both tremendous privilege as well as enormous responsibilities. It is on a smaller scale to what you face, that is true, but it is still similar."

"What would you have me do, then?" Menelaus spat, clearly finished with the conversation.

"I would have you cleave to your wife. I would have you apologize to her, beg her forgiveness, and do whatever you can to reconcile. I would have you stop your infidelities and genuinely seek to make your wife happy."

"You would have me humble myself?" Menelaus asked incredulously. "That would be humiliating after all these years."

"Can one really apologize and reconcile without humility?"

Menelaus shook his head. "I cannot do that. I will not do that. I would be miserable."

"Healing your marriage would make you miserable?"

Menelaus sighed heavily. "There's nothing to heal!" he exclaimed. "We never loved each other. We never liked each other. Hell, I don't think we ever even respected each other. There is nothing to heal or fix because there was never anything between us worth salvaging in the first place."

"Very well. Why not rebuild everything anew?"

"Because it displeases me!" Menelaus shouted. "I would sooner divorce her and let her live her life as she pleases than ever try and please her myself."

"You want her to be miserable?" Odysseus asked, eyebrows furrowed in confusion. "More than that, you want to be the reason for her misery?"

"Yes," Menelaus said, glaring at him. "It is the only thing which comforts me."

Odysseus was utterly shocked. He stared at Menelaus, eyes wide in disbelief, for several moments. He did not know what to say or think. He eventually stood, leaving his brandy and unfinished cigar on the table.

"Where are you going?" Menelaus asked.

"I am leaving," he said. "And in the morning, Penelope and I will begin our return to Ithaca."

Menelaus stood and held out his arms in an exasperated shrug. "Why?"

"Because I cannot stay here. I cannot support you when I know you feel this way."

The king's eyes flashed with anger and pain. "So you are abandoning me as well?"

"I do not abandon you, Menelaus. You have chosen a path that I wholeheartedly condemn, and while I will always consider you one of my closest friends, I cannot in good conscience stay here when you hold such dishonor in your heart."

"Dishonor?" Menelaus exclaimed, raising his voice. "You are accusing your king of dishonor?"

"I am. Openly and without shame." He let out a slow breath. "I have defended you at every opportunity to do so, and believe me, Menelaus, there have been many. Do you even know how many of your subjects wish for you to sign the treaty? Do you know how many condemn you for your bloodlust and warmongering?"

Menelaus stood, eyes wide with anger, but he did not respond.

"And though I agreed with them, I still stood forward and defended you because I believed, in my heart, that you were following what you believed was the right course of action. Now I must face the truth."

"And what is that?"

Odysseus met his gaze. "That you have only refused to sign the treaty to spite your wife. That you have cost Greece the lives of too many of her men, and that you did so not out of personal conviction, but personal pleasure. That, in fact, you have been and continue to be unfaithful to your wife not because it is your right as the king, but because you know it causes her pain. And that the decency, honor, and integrity you once possessed have been replaced by a selfishness akin to a child's tantrum." He shook his head. "I must face the reality that you are not the king I though you were." He almost left then but stopped. "You are not the *man* I thought you were."

He said nothing else. He simply bowed and left the study, his heart heavy. He had always known that there was no love between the king and queen, but he had never imagined that Menelaus could treat anyone with such contempt and cruelty. Odysseus had watched Helen over dinner and he had seen how deep her heartache went. It wasn't that she had loved Menelaus and been rejected. It went deeper than that. She had, to Odysseus's eyes, given up everything she had ever wanted for Menelaus, only to find herself adrift and alone, without recourse, married to a man who seemed to thoroughly hate her. Indeed, Menelaus seemed content to waste his reign, his power, his influence; he had changed into someone Odysseus did not recognize, and that was what disappointed Odysseus most acutely.

He reached the bed chamber he shared with Penelope and began to undress, his mind full of too much. He thought of the many servants and tenants he had lost over the course of the war, how many families that no longer had fathers, brothers, and sons. He thought of Achilles and Patroclus, two of his closest friends who could be called to the front lines in a moment's notice if things worsened with Troy. He thought of Penelope and his heart panged. What evils might she have to face in the coming years? Greece needed a united king and queen. Even if they did not love each other, they needed to be on the same side. Odysseus thought that Helen was the one willing to do that work; she had proven as much when she confronted Menelaus on the need for a peace treaty with Troy. She must have known he would not listen, and yet she had tried all the same. Menelaus, on the other hand, refused to listen to anyone on some misguided sense of personal pride. He would lead to the downfall of all of Greece.

Odysseus swore he would not let that happen.

CHAPTER TWENTY-FIVE

A Duchess and The Queen

The two women were quiet as they began their stroll through the gardens. Penelope was delighted by the garden and its many varieties of flowers, trees, shrubs. She complimented the queen on how well tended everything was. She was fond of her own gardens, of course, and wondered if the queen and she might bond over a shared love of gardening. It was not to be, though. Helen seemed to have no interest in plants. They settled into an awkward silence as they continued to stroll, and Penelope tried desperately to think of something to say. She wanted to be a friend to this woman, but how could she? Helen was older than Penelope by some years, and her position was far superior to Penelope's. What could she possible say to raise a queen's spirits?

"What is it like?" Helen asked Penelope suddenly.

"What is what like, Your Highness?"

"Being in a happy marriage."

Penelope was not sure how to respond. She did not wish to add insult to injury for this woman who so clearly longed for some form of kindness and respect from her husband. But nor could she lie or avoid the question now that it had been asked.

"I confess myself hesitant to answer your question, Your Highness," she said.

Helen smiled. "You are not going to anger me, dear," she said. "I simply want to live vicariously through you. That is all."

Penelope nodded slowly. "In answering your question, then, I must say that I have never known so much happiness. Odysseus is attentive and kind and gentle. I am fortunate, indeed."

"You were not in love when you married?" asked the queen. "Forgive my impertinence, but I understood from Menelaus that you were not."

Penelope cleared her throat, thoroughly unprepared for such questions. "No, we were not in love yet. I do believe we were on our way to being so. We admired each other, to be sure, and were, of course, attracted to each other."

Helen nodded slowly, seemingly deep in thought. "And do you know when that love bloomed in full?"

Penelope did know when her love for Odysseus had been fully realized, but she wasn't about to confess to it, especially not to the queen of all Greece. The young woman hesitated, wondering what to say or how to describe their morning in the woods when they had gone hunting without giving explicit details.

"I suppose...it came on gradually," she said, though that was a lie.

"I may not know what a loving marriage looks like, my dear, but I can spot a liar when they are telling me an untruth."

Penelope turned her gaze on the queen. "Forgive me Your Highness. I am not trying to be deceitful. It is just that...well, the matter is a delicate one, if you know what I mean."

Helen's eyes sparkled suddenly and she nodded her head slowly, a small smile tugging at the corners of her mouth. "Aha, so I see. Well, rest easy darling. You are already married to the duke so you cannot be faulted for anything you may or may not have done before your wedding. And the gods know I will certainly never judge any woman for using her own body in whatever manner she so desires. As long as it was consensual..." she raised her eyebrows, clearly asking Penelope to confirm.

"It was, very much so, Your Highness," she said.

"Then I will never judge or shame you." She let out a sigh. "So," she said, smiling wryly, "the pure and righteous Penelope Auckland Halstead is not so pure and righteous as has been believed."

Penelope blushed. Helen laughed.

"Do not be so forlorn, my dear. I think it's a very good thing."

"You do?" Penelope asked, frowning.

"I do. Women are afforded very few comforts in this life. If you were able to find real, true pleasure before marrying a man with so much power, then I celebrate that with you. The gods know we deserve so much better than what we are given."

Penelope's heart panged for the queen. She seemed a truly good, honorable, caring woman who had been dealt one of the worst hands anyone could imagine.

"Has he changed his behavior since the wedding?" Helen asked.

"No, Your Highness. He is just as attentive and loving now as he was before our wedding day. More so, even."

"Good. That is how it should be." They were quiet then and Penelope felt it only right to let the queen lead whatever conversation it was they were having. "I almost loved Menelaus once," she said at last. "There was one afternoon mere days before our wedding when he seemed to look upon me with tenderness rather than resentment. I cannot even recall what the circumstances were now, but he found me crying here in this garden and he held me." She smiled. "He made no promises. He professed no love, and yet his touch was gentle. At that moment I dared to believe that we could make something good out of the wretched betrothal." She sighed. "We did consummate the marriage. And though I knew he did not love me, he did more than I expected he would to ensure that I enjoyed the wedding night."

"But it...wasn't enough to constitute love or affection?" Penelope asked.

Helen shook her head. "No. Not for him, anyway. If he had continued in that way, I think things might have been different. But he did not and soon was seeking out the pleasures of other women instead." She looked at Penelope. "I sincerely hope that you never have to face the kind of heartbreak that comes from feeling your own husband despise you."

Penelope didn't think such a thing would ever happen with her and Odysseus. Her smile must have communicated that thought because Helen started to chuckle.

"You think your marriage immune to such things, I see."

"No, Your Highness, that is not –"

"Yes it is. And why should you not? You are both in love with one another so of course you believe yourselves immune to the usual hardships of marital life." She stared at Penelope. "You have love for each other now, it is true. But love does not withstand everything."

"Doesn't it?" Penelope heard herself ask.

"If only it did, sweet one. Let us hope the duke does not neglect your marriage. Let us hope the attentiveness he shows you continues and that the happiness you now possess continues. You may still face problems, all couples do, but at least you will be confident in your husband's affection for you."

She patted Penelope's arm then and they continued walking, but Penelope was lost in thought. She couldn't tell if the queen's last comments had been prayers of hopefulness, or declarations of doubt. She wasn't sure she wanted to know, either.

CHAPTER TWENTY-SIX
A King's Thoughts

Menelaus sat and stared at the crackling flames. He was more angry than he had ever been in his life. His hands shook. His mind raced. He wanted to shout or throw over a table or punch someone. He had never expected that Odysseus, his oldest friend, would ever have spoken to him in such a manner, and the conversation had him fuming. But not at Odysseus. Not really. The man had only spoken his mind, and that was something Menelaus had always loved about him. Odysseus Halstead never lied or told him what he wanted to hear. No, he was not mad at his friend. He was not even mad at Helen, he soon realized.

He was mad at himself.

How much of what he had said to Odysseus had been deflection, he wondered? Even he did not know, for it had been some time now since he had last allowed himself to feel the truth of his reality. His marriage with Helen had always been a thorn in his side, that much was true, but he had lied when he said that it pleased him to make her miserable. He did not love Helen. He had never loved Helen. But he did admire her, and he did desire her good opinion. She was an intelligent and capable woman with more personal strength than he had ever possessed in his entire life.

He had not told Odysseus the details of their first year and a half of marriage, memories that filled Menelaus with conflicting emotions. Those first months had been the hardest, but also the most tender, the most promising. They had agreed that even though neither of them wanted the marriage, they would do what they could to make it work. The fate of Greece depended on it, and neither of them needed to be told of the importance of their success.

He had not told Odysseus, nor anyone, of the feelings he had developed for Helen over the course of those eighteen months. He had not quite made it to love, but he had grown to respect, admire, and care for her profoundly. She had become an intimate friend and confidant, someone he trusted, someone whose opinion he sought regularly because he could always count on her seeing things in such a way that guided him in the right direction. Indeed, he believed with his whole heart that he would have come to love her had those first sixteen months not also brought with them tremendous loss.

Hardly anyone knew about the three miscarriages. And no one but the midwives knew about the stillborn son. Tears filled Menelaus' eyes as he remembered Helen's screams, her wails of heartbreak and disappointment. She had been despondent, unreachable. For days, she had travailed, refusing to eat or drink anything. He had held her. He had done his best to comfort her, even as he, too, grieved their loss.

It had been too much. Nothing he did helped, and he was afraid that he would have to watch her fade away to nothing, and so he had done the only thing he could think to do: he left her alone.

He knew now what a mistake that had been. Hell, he had known then, but his heart had not been strong enough to support her. He could not watch her grieve, knowing he was helpless to do anything. Against his better judgment, he sought his own solace in the arms of another woman. He was ashamed to admit it, but the relief she had afforded him had been tremendous. He told himself it would only last until Helen had recovered, if she ever did. But by the time their third anniversary had passed, Menelaus had conceived two illegitimate children with this other woman. And really, even that would not have been so bad, except for one moment in time that Menelaus now regretted with every breath he took.

Helen had seen him with the woman and their two children.

That was the moment when the fate of their marriage had been sealed, and there was nothing he could do to change course, to reverse the movement of time, fold back the years and undo the choices that lead him to that moment. Helen had been heartbroken again, only then it was over something he could have avoided if he had been less selfish. For all his talk of Helen's betrayals and insufficiencies, the truth was that she had always been the perfect wife and queen.

He was the one found wanting.

And that was the real reason he resented her. Not for any failing on her part, but on his own. She was the reflection of the kind of ruler and spouse he should have been, and failed. Menelaus stood to his feet and began to pace. Odysseus' words rang in his ears: "You're not the man I thought you were." Had they been spoken by anyone else, Menelaus could have shrugged them off, ignored them, denied their validity, but from Odysseus, they sunk deep into his heart and planted roots. He knew he had to make a choice. He could either persist in his present course and lose not only his friendship with Odysseus, but the love and admiration of all his people, or he could listen to Helen and his advisors and sign the treaty with Troy.

He hated to sign the treaty with Troy. He had not begun the war, but he had sworn to his father when he was young that he would finish it, and a treaty was not what he had meant. Still, he could see that Greece would not withstand more of this half-hearted conflict. Yes, for the sake of his country and of his throne, he had to sign the treaty. It would eat him alive, but at least he would still live to finish out his days as King.

But that wasn't enough, he told himself. He had to reconcile with Helen. He had to humble himself, and by the gods, it had to be a low humbling, indeed. How many years had he been unfaithful now? How many women had he known? How many illegitimate children had he conceived? He had to humble himself lower and lower for every failing, every choice he made that had ever caused Helen a single moment of regret. Could he do that? Did he even want to?

No, he didn't want to. Not even a little. But he wanted to lose his country even less. For some time now he had been worried that Helen would take drastic measures to escape their marriage, to escape *him*, and if that happened, Greece could split into a civil war. That meant there must be a radical change in his attitudes, behaviors, and perspectives. He was truly sorry for the many choices he'd made over the last decade or more, and while he still dreaded the idea of humbling himself, he knew this was important. Perhaps fatally so. He racked his brain to think of anything he could do to make up for the affairs and soon, he had a list. This was the celebration of his marriage, after all, and Helen deserved to be praised for the many amazing things she had done as his queen. That was a fact he would not dispute.

Yes, he thought, he would start there. He couldn't profess any kind of love for her, nor could he promise to do so in the future. He believed too much time had passed and too many harsh words had been spoken for that to ever be realistic. But he could at least give an honest accounting of all the ways she had made his reign better, and he knew just how to do so.

He grabbed a piece of parchment and began to write down the announcement that he wanted to be read the next morning before the tournament. It would also be written on parchment with the official royal seal and distributed to everyone in Sparta as a pamphlet highlighting Helen's accomplishments in her many years as queen. It was not enough, but it was a start, one he hoped would begin the process of making amends.

Once he had finished his announcement and passed on the instructions to his primary royal advisor, he sat to write a letter to Odysseus, begging him to stay at least a fortnight. He acknowledged his friend's accusations and admitted that he was correct in his assessments. Menelaus swore to Odysseus that he would do better, that he would try to be the husband Helen deserved, though he didn't know if she would accept his efforts. He then emphasized how much he wanted Odysseus to stay, gave the letter to his butler to deliver to Odysseus' room, and then Menelaus finally retired to his own bed chamber. He gave instructions for fresh flowers to be left on the table in Helen's room in the morning, and then climbed into bed, exhausted.

CHAPTER TWENTY-SEVEN

A Queen's Hope

Helen lay in bed for some time after she awoke, having neither the will nor the interest in climbing from under the warm covers. Any time she argued with Menelaus left her drained and melancholy. She had hoped that, even without affection, Menelaus would come to respect and trust her in matters of state, and instead he despised her. Perhaps even more so now than he ever had previously.

She covered her head with her blankets and tried to fight the sudden tears that filled her eyes. Why did she care about Menelaus or what he thought of her? She didn't know. But it had been so long since she had felt anything even remotely akin to tenderness from her husband. He did not care about her or the many ways in which he inflicted pain and heartache. And yet she still harbored desires for his good opinion, though she could not think why.

A knock sounded at her door and a moment later her ladies in waiting entered. She climbed from bed, her head pounding and tight from lack of sleep. She stood and walked over to where she would be dressed, but stopped suddenly when she saw the bouquet of lilies on her table. It was enormous with at least forty lilies surrounded by smaller white flowers she couldn't name. She furrowed her eyebrows.

"Who left those?" she asked.

"His Majesty instructed us to bring them in when we came to dress you, Your Highness," said her lead lady in waiting, a woman named Carissa.

Helen was stunned into silence. Menelaus had never given her flowers in all the years they had been married. He had never given her any gifts. Yet here was a stunning bouquet of her favorite flower sent from him. How did he even know what her favorite flower was? Was it possible this was someone else's doing? It had to be.

Was this meant to be a cruel joke, she thought as her ladies dressed her. A manipulation? She didn't know, but it gnawed at her, distracted her, rolled over in her mind again and again. It did not make sense. It was impossible that Menelaus had sent the flowers simply as a kind gesture. There had to be some other ulterior motive, though she knew not what it could be.

The day was going to be full of events. She would spend the bulk of it next to Menelaus and so had to steel herself to his whispered jabs and jokes. She decided that she would, at least, look as beautiful as she was able, and so instead of wearing her usual gown of red and gold, she instructed her ladies to grab the more attractive gown of purple satin trimmed in silver. The bodice was tight and cut low, revealing her still beautiful figure and ample bosom. Instead of wearing her hair up as she usually did, she instructed them to let her long black curls hang low down her back. For jewelry she chose her official queen's jewels:

her crown, earrings, and necklace of diamonds crested in pure, Spartan silver. Each piece sparkled brightly against the deep brown of her skin. She smiled softly at herself. If Menelaus wasn't going to try to make her feel special, then she would do so herself.

She breakfasted alone in her private breakfast room and then immediately made her way to the tourney grounds at the back of the castle. She met Menelaus in the hall. He saw her coming towards him and immediately straightened his posture and smiled awkwardly. He seemed uncomfortable. Helen didn't know why he would, and then remembered the flowers. She approached him and curtsied.

"You're looking well this morning, Your Majesty," she said in her usual greeting.

As she rose she saw that his eyes were staring down at her bosom and she felt herself blush.

"You look…" he started and then stopped, as though searching for the right word. His eyes kept fluttering up to meet hers and then back down to look at her bosom. He cleared his throat. "You look absolutely beautiful," he said, his eyes roaming up her form until he met her gaze. "Truly."

She smiled. "Thank you, Your Majesty."

"I trust you received the flowers this morning?" he asked.

She nodded. "I did, indeed. And I thank you for them. Lilies are my favorite."

He smiled. "Yes, I remembered. I am glad you enjoyed them."

He held out his hand and she took it, the two of them entering the tourney yard where already many hundreds, if not thousands, of spectators had gathered to watch. They all cheered as their king and queen came into sight and Helen waved. Next to her, Menelaus seemed tense.

"Are you alright, Your Majesty?" she asked. Normally she wouldn't have made any inquiry, but his demeanor was distracting and made her uneasy.

He smiled over at her. "Yes, perfectly so. Thank you."

The trumpeters on either side of their dais sounded the royal call and the king's royal announcer stepped up to his podium.

"Good people of Sparta," he began, his voice carrying across the tourney yard, "we have all gathered here to celebrate the marriage of our King, Menelaus the Brave, to our Queen, Helen the Beautiful!" Everyone cheered. "But before the knights take their places, his most honorable majesty, King Menelaus, has an announcement dedicated to his beloved queen and wife!"

Silence spread across the yard and Helen felt her heart begin to race. She turned and looked at Menelaus, her eyebrows furrowed. Was this what had made him so nervous? Was he about to humiliate her? Had the flowers been a ruse to lower her guard? He met her stare and she searched his eyes for some sign of malicious intent, but she saw nothing.

"These are the words of the King: Queen Helen has been by His Majesty's side for many years," the announcer continued. "She has devoted herself utterly to his benefit and, through him, the benefit of all of Greece. If not for her, His Majesty would have lost himself to the demands of the crown, decimating all of who he is and all he ever dreamed to be. It is her strength and not his that has sustained this great country throughout the ongoing war with Troy, and it is her honest words to him in moments of great anxiety that have kept him steady and focused on what is best for his people."

Helen felt her heart would pound out of her chest. She didn't understand any of this. Were these truly Menelaus' words? Did he mean them honestly? She didn't know and the more she listened, the more she felt her heartbeat in her temples.

"In fact, it is to Queen Helen that we are all indebted, for her insight, her courage in bringing her honest perspectives to the king in the most dire moments are what have shown him the reality of the war with Troy. His Majesty has, therefore, resolved to sign the –" The announcer froze and looked to the king for assurance to continue, assurance Menelaus granted with a nod. "...resolved to sign the projected treaty with Troy, ending the war once and for all!"

A great roar lifted into the air. Helen felt as though the very breath in her lungs had been stolen on the wind. She heard nothing else. She heard only the thunderous sound of her own heart clapping along with the applause within the stadium. She was dizzy and overwhelmed and stood to leave. Menelaus called after her, but she heard not a word. Her eyes were full of tears as she made her way back into the hall.

"Helen?" Menelaus asked and took her hand, calling her focus back to the present.

She looked down at his hand and then back up at his face.

"You have not touched me in years," she said, her voice no louder than a whisper.

He did not speak, but he moved closer. Tears were streaming down her face, though she hardly noticed.

"Did you...not like it?" he asked.

She shook her head. "I do not even know what that was," she said, breathing deeply to try and calm herself, but to no avail. "I do not know..." her voice trailed off.

She felt she was nearing a state of panic. She did not understand what was happening, or why Menelaus had allowed such an announcement to be given, for surely they could not have been his real words. Her heart would not accept that. It had to be someone else's doing, likely Odysseus'. And yet, Menelaus stood before her now, his eyes full of so many emotions she hadn't felt from him in years.

She shook her head. "No, I must go," she said, turning to leave.

"Helen, please," he said, taking her other hand.

She looked at him but could hardly see him through the onslaught of tears. Her breathing was fast as sobs crashed over her, so much pain and torment coming to the surface after years of repression.

"I have been an absolute brute," he said, staring into her eyes. "I know I am no great romantic and at best I have been an indifferent husband, but please, I wish you to accept the flowers and the announcement that was just read as the beginning stages of my apology."

She furrowed her eyebrows. "Apology? I...what..."

"Yes. I know you have no reason to trust me, and I do not ask you to. But for the sake of Greece, I wish you to believe me to be sincere."

She couldn't speak. She could hardly breathe now.

"I want this tournament to celebrate something real," Menelaus continued, "and, while our marriage has been anything but, I cannot ignore the very many ways in which you have supported me, trusted me, helped me, and guided me. Those things I can acknowledge, and should have done a long time ago."

Helen stared unblinking, as he lifted both of her hands to his lips and kissed them. His own eyes glistened with tears now.

"Did..." Her voice cracked and she had to clear it before she could continue. "Did you mean what was said in the announcement?"

Menelaus nodded and smiled. "I did. Every word of it."

"Including the treaty?"

He nodded again. "Yes. I won't deny that I am not happy with that choice, but I believe it to be the right one."

Helen was, again, overwhelmed. She couldn't speak. More tears streamed down her face. For some reason, she didn't know why, he stepped closer and held her hands to his chest.

"I know that it will take more than this to convince you how sorry I am, but it is important to me that you know that I am trying." He gave a sad smile. "I am sorry that it has taken me this long to do what I should have always done. And more than anything, Helen, I am sorry that I abandoned you in your darkest moments and sought the love of another woman."

Helen felt her heart shatter. She knew he was referring to the mistress he had taken after their son had been stillborn. How long had she waited to hear these words? How fervently had she prayed to Eros for something, anything, even remotely tender from Menelaus in the years since that great loss? And now he was speaking the words she had given up all hope of ever hearing.

"This is Odysseus' doing," she said, shaking her head, feeling herself unable to accept that this was really her husband's choice.

"No, it is not. He spoke honest words to me, Helen," Menelaus said, trying to keep her gaze locked on his. "But the flowers, the announcement, and the choice to sign the treaty are mine alone." He looked down for a moment and then up at her. "And they are the beginning of what I hope will be a new start to this marriage. If that is something you desire, of course."

Helen could stand no more of this. She simply smiled at Menelaus and curtsied, excusing herself to her chamber to cry. He called after her, but she did not stop, and he did not follow. She had a limited amount of time to compose herself before the tourney began, but she needed those moments by herself. She needed to release some of the emotional pressure before returning into the public eye. She was glad that Menelaus let her go, and wished she could have expressed her gratitude in that moment, but words would not come. Not yet. He had done something she believed was impossible.

He had given her hope.

CHAPTER TWENTY-EIGHT

Nearing a State of Panic

Penelope breakfasted alone. When she awoke, Odysseus was not in the room. She wasn't worried; she knew he was probably with the king, having been so long since they had last had the chance to spend time with one another. But as the morning grew long and it came closer to the start of the tourney, Penelope felt herself growing anxious. It wasn't like Odysseus to disappear for this long without leaving a message for her. Still, she told herself not to worry. If she had to go to the tourney alone for now, then so be it.

Another hour passed and Odysseus still had not appeared. She was miffed that Odysseus hadn't left word of where he would be, but she refused to let it dampen her enjoyment of the events for the day. She had never been to an official royal tourney and was very much looking forward to it. She invited her lady's maid, Grace, to attend with her, and the two women walked down the hall towards the tourney grounds.

The stadium was already packed with people. Penelope and Odysseus had been given seats down in front of the dais where the king and queen would sit. She and Grace took their seats, asked a cup bearer for some wine, and then settled in to wait for the beginning of the tourney. Penelope tried to distract herself by talking to Grace and some of the other attendees, but she couldn't help but feel as though something was going on, something she should know about. It made her fidgety. She nearly spilled red wine all over her pale day dress.

"Are you alright, my lady?" asked Grace

Penelope smiled and nodded. "Yes, I am just distracted today."

The king and queen arrived then, sending everyone into a roar of applause. And to Penelope's great surprise, the king's royal announcer gave a speech written by the king for the queen. Penelope expected such a thing to be generic and insincere, considering the argument she and Odysseus had overheard between the royal couple the night before, but6 it was the opposite. The speech was heartfelt and praised Helen for a number of things, all of which Penelope felt were most deserved. And to make it even better, the speech ended with the announcement of the king's intentions to sign a treaty with Troy.

Penelope was shocked beyond anything she could express. How could the man she had heard shouting at his wife only the night before, the man who had been unfaithful for nearly the entirety of his marriage, write something like this? She wondered if Odysseus had something to do with it, and her heart fluttered. She liked the idea of her husband scolding the king who had been acting like a petulant child, although she was certain that anything Odysseus said would never have been an actual scolding. Still, the idea made her smile.

Just then, Odysseus appeared next to her.

"There you are," she said as he took a seat beside her. "I was beginning to worry."

"I am sorry, my dear," he said, looking around almost frantically.

Penelope furrowed her eyebrows. "Are you alright?"

He nodded and took the wine glass from her hand. "Come with me," he said, taking her hand and pulling her away from their seats.

"The tourney is just –"

But he did not respond. He simply pulled her along. She motioned for Grace to stay where she was, and then turned back towards Odysseus as they walked back into the palace and down the hall. She tried to get him to stop and talk to her, but he would not. Her heart was racing as they went all the way back to their chamber.

"Odysseus," she said breathlessly as he shut the door behind them, "what on earth is the matter with you?"

He was pacing and seemed out of sorts.

"You left me alone all morning without a word, and now you pull me away from the tourney without explanation, leaving Grace by herself."

He faced her then, his eyes full of unspoken emotion. He stared at her a moment without speaking and then immediately went to her and wrapped her in a tight embrace.

"Odysseus!" she exclaimed, feeling herself growing more upset. "Please, I need you to explain –"

"I am sorry," he said, looking down at her. "I awoke early intending for us to leave before the tourney even began, but found that Menelaus was already outside our room. He asked to speak with me and I have been reeling ever since."

He smiled and laughed and Penelope furrowed her eyebrows. "Why would you take us away so soon?"

"I told Menelaus last night that if he was going to treat his wife the way he did in the argument we overheard, that I couldn't stay and support him."

Penelope raised her eyebrows. So he had scolded the king after all. "You did?"

Odysseus nodded. "And this morning he talked with me more about it. He told me he had left flowers for Helen on her table and he showed me what he had written for his announcement, and..." He chuckled and looked up at the ceiling. "He actually told me that he would never be unfaithful to Helen again."

Penelope smiled. "Well, I can understand why you are so giddy, at least."

"That is not even the best part," he said, his eyes flashing with excitement. "He wants me to be his chief of counsel."

Penelope felt her heart thunder in her chest. She raised her eyebrows. "He...He said this?"

Odysseus nodded. "Yes! He said that he needs me here. I am the person he respects the most and he relies on me and my advice."

"Surely he can simply write to you and ask for your opinion on matters as they arise?" she asked.

He shrugged. "He could, but he would prefer to have me here."

Penelope felt herself nearing a state of panic. She did not want this, that much she knew for certain. Living within the palace was fine temporarily, but she couldn't stand it if it was her permanent residence. She far preferred their home in the country, and had every intention of going back to that home once the tournament was over.

"And with the coming treaty, he will need us even more," he said. "I will write to Barnes and Mrs. Smith today and have them pack up the rest of your clothes and send them here. And I will have to ensure that Baxter has enough help to look after the tenants and the rest of the workers. But all of that can be done later. I brought you here to celebrate." He pressed a kiss to her forehead and moved to pour her a glass of wine.

"Odysseus," she said, trying to keep herself calm. "I can see that you are excited by this prospect, but you have not yet asked me if this is something I want."

He looked up at her, confused. "What do you mean?"

"Did it not occur to you that this plan of living in Sparta might be something you should consult me about first before you made any definitive decisions?"

He could only shrug. "I thought you would be pleased."

"Why? Coming here to celebrate your friend's marriage is one thing. Moving here when we have already begun to build a life back in Ithaca is something else entirely."

"I didn't think anything of the move," he said, visibly deflating. "I thought this would be an incredible advancement for us."

"For us?" she asked. "Or for you?"

He stared at her, unblinking, and so she continued, her heart racing. They had never fought before, and it seemed that now would be the moment when they broke that pattern.

"My father lives in Ithaca and is an old man. I do not want to live so far away from him when he has few years left of life. And should we have any children in the coming years, I want them to know their only living grandparent as more than a shadowy face they saw once in their infancy." She felt herself growing angry and tried to keep calm, but it took a great deal of effort. "My friends all live in Ithaca. Am I never to see them? Never to be involved in their lives? Never to be truly acquainted with their spouses and children?"

Odysseus said nothing.

"I know no one here besides you. I have no purpose here outside of you. In Ithaca, I am the mistress of an estate. I have a position of importance that I can use to do a great deal of good for the people within your dukedom."

"Are you telling me no?" he asked, his voice flat and emotionless.

"I am telling you that *I* will not be living in Sparta."

The darkness of anger fell over his features. "You are dictating this to me?"

Stubbornness rose up within her. "You dictated to me that we would be moving here, did you not?"

"That is different," he said, walking towards her. "I am a duke."

"And I am a duchess."

"I am your husband!"

"And I am your wife!"

They were silent for some moments. Penelope forced herself to remain stoic, to hide the tears that continually threatened to fill her eyes. She would not waver here. She would not falter. This was something she could not compromise on.

"I am not telling you what to do," she said. "I am only explaining what I intend to do. And if this is, indeed, the course of action you decide to take, then I shall return to Ithaca on my own and look after the estate in your absence."

"I will not live here without my wife at my side," he said through grit teeth.

She shrugged. "That is your problem to figure out then, is it not?" She turned and grabbed hold of the door handle, and then looked over her shoulder at Odysseus. "You can scold the king for treating his wife with less respect than she deserves, but you see not the same pattern in your own actions?"

Penelope did not wait for him to respond. She simply turned and left the chamber.

Chapter Twenty-Nine

How Close

Odysseus watched Penelope walk away and felt himself flush with anger. He wanted to follow her, but he forced himself to stay in the bedroom. He didn't understand why she was upset. He thought she would be genuinely excited for such an opportunity; she would get to live in Sparta, one of the most luxurious and popular cities in Greece; she would be friends with the queen; she would have more luxury than ever would have been possible in Ithaca. He had truly thought she would be ecstatic, and now didn't know what to do or say. She did not want to stay in Sparta. And he did not want to be in Sparta without her. Anger pulsed through him for several minutes. He paced the room, thinking over their conversation, looking for anything he could use to convince her to stay.

It took half an hour before he realized that he was never going to convince her to stay. She had been adamant. And that meant he was going to have to make a difficult choice. She was right: this was his issue to resolve. He had not asked her before making up his mind to accept the king's request, and that was entirely on him. Had he done so, he would have known how she felt before getting his own hopes up. He did not like the guilt he felt that he had not only insulted Penelope by refusing to give her a say in such an important matter, but also that he had disrespected her by not even considering that her opinion was important in the first place. How could he have not considered her? She would have considered him if their roles had been reversed, he knew that beyond a doubt.

Moreover, she was right that his behavior mirrored the king's. Had not Odysseus just scolded the king the night before on how disrespectful it was for him to focus solely on his own desires rather than those of his wife? What good were those words now if he did not apply the same standard to his own marriage? He felt foolish. He was angry, only now he was angry more at himself than anything else. Perhaps if he had spoken to Penelope about it all, she might have been willing to consider staying with him in Sparta, but now those hopes seemed dashed.

The guilt he felt softened the anger. He had caused this whole debacle, and he couldn't deny it. He sat on the edge of the bed and covered his face with his hands. He would not make her stay with him. He would not manipulate her or argue with her or try to change her mind, either. If she did not want to stay in Sparta, then he would respect that. It was only right, considering that he had essentially asked her to give up all of her hopes and dreams for the sake of his. What kind of marriage would they have if he continued to press the matter?

She would return to Ithaca and he would remain in Sparta.

At first he thought that perhaps they really could make it work living apart, but that idea did not last long. They were trying to have a child, after all, and how would they accomplish that if they were not living together? Moreover, even if she did get pregnant, did he want to miss the raising of his heir, his flesh and blood? The gods knew his own father had barely been in his life as a child, and he did not want to perpetuate the same kind of loneliness for his own progeny. But even more than that, would he be happy without Penelope at his side and sharing his bed? Would she be happy without him in Ithaca?

He groaned and ran his hands through his hair. It was clear that he had to turn down the king's offer, although it pained him to admit it. He wanted to take the position. He wanted to live in Sparta. He wanted to be close to Menelaus, one of his oldest friends. But he couldn't sacrifice the other desires of his heart for those things. It upset him to know that he had to choose between the two, but he also knew whom he would choose in the end. It didn't matter how many scenarios or justifications he played in his mind, he would not live apart from Penelope. He could, as her husband, force her to stay, but he would never do that. So he had to choose.

And he chose her.

It was astonishing how easily he had made up his mind. Odysseus really had wanted to accept the position offered to him by the king, but once he had decided to decline it, all excitement for the prospect faded. All disappointment faded. It was as though the king's offer had not been important to him at all, especially in light of the hopes he had for himself and Penelope, and now he wondered how he ever could have made such a mistake? What had blinded him? He did not know. Perhaps it was the excitement to be reunited with his oldest friend.

Perhaps it was the bustle of the city. Whatever it was, its influence had faded and Odysseus knew that his truest desire, his deepest wish, was to live out his days with Penelope and any children they might have. He would still write to Menelaus. He might even visit from time to time, in moments of dire need, but he would not live in Sparta permanently.

Now, all that remained was to speak to his wife and repair the damage he had caused. He left the room and made his way back to the tourney grounds where he believed Penelope had gone. And, indeed, she was there, but she was still in the hallway. She had not returned to her seat. As he approached he saw that she was crying. He quickened his pace, his heart melting at the sight of his beloved wife in turmoil.

"Penelope," he said, reaching out for her hand.

She saw him and turned away, intending to go out to the stadium, but he took her hand before she could walk through the door.

"I do not wish to see or speak to you at the moment," she said, her voice thick with tears.

"I'm not going to take the position," he said.

She turned to face him. "What?"

He smiled softly. "I do want to take it. Or, at least, I did before. But I will not force you to stay here, and if you are going back to Ithaca, then that is where I am going, too."

"Odysseus, I don't want you to resent me –"

"I was the one who accepted a position without asking your opinion first. I cannot resent you for a failing that was mine." He smiled. "Besides, I want children, and we cannot exactly raise a family together if we are not together, can we?"

She smiled softly. "That is what I want as well."

He nodded. "Good. I will likely travel back and forth between here and Ithaca. Menelaus does need me, and I intend to be there when I can. But I will not live here long term. Is that acceptable?"

She nodded. "Yes, it is. Very much so. As long as I might come with you, from time to time? I believe the queen is fond of my company, and I should like to be of use to her if I can."

Odysseus smiled. "I think that is a wonderful idea."

He wrapped his arms around her and held her close. She smelled like lavender and honeysuckle, and gods, he wanted to have her right there. It had been days since they had last joined their bodies and he was aching for her. He felt his arousal heighten at the thought and almost instantly, he began to harden.

"Odysseus," Penelope said, pulling away only slightly, "I believe you are what is considered indecent for the public eye," she said, looking down at his growing erection and then back up at him.

He grinned. "It has been a while since we last enjoyed one another. I cannot help it."

She looked around for a moment and then smiled up at him. "We could try here? Now?"

He raised his eyebrows. "Someone could walk by."

She nodded her head to a darker corner a few feet away. "No one will see us there. Not if we're quick."

He didn't need another invitation. He pressed his lips against hers, pulled her against his chest, and then made his way to the shadowed corner of the hallway. Her fingers worked at the front of his trousers to undo the fall and, once it fell open, she reached her hand in and began to stroke him gently, oh so very gently, hardly touching him at all, and yet it was enough to make his head spin with desire.

He bunched the skirt of her dress up above her knees, lifted her body up to his and slowly slid himself inside of her. Her own arousal was dripping. He let out a groan, which she promptly shushed, and he smiled.

"I've never done this in a public place before," he said, throbbing against the inside of her.

"Neither have I," she said, pulling him in with her legs that she had wrapped around his waist. "For the love of Aphrodite, please, Odysseus, fuck me already."

He didn't need to be asked twice. He rocked his hips back and forth, his lips pressed against hers. She was quiet, barely making any noise at all, as he pulled and shoved himself out of and back into her. Gods, he loved this woman. He stopped his thrusts as an idea came into his mind. He smiled, pulled out of her and just as she was about to ask what he was doing, he went down on his knees and wrapped his lips around the sensitive flesh between her legs.

He didn't know how long he was there, his tongue sliding back and forth, and he didn't care. She deserved happiness and pleasure, and he wanted to give those things to her. He smiled as she quickly reached a climax, but he did not stop. He would not stop. Not unless she told him to.

"Odysseus," she whispered breathlessly, "what...are you..."

"I want you to have it again," he said, and then continued to work his tongue around her.

Moans she had previously been able to keep quiet now were slightly louder. He didn't care about that, either. They were married. What kind of consequences could there possibly be? An idea came to him then and he slowly slid one of his fingers into her and gently moved it in and out as his tongue continued to slide back and forth ever so gently.

"I'm...oh, gods...I'm...I'm..."

She sucked in a gasping breath as climax rolled over her again and her body began to quiver against its weight. But Odysseus still wasn't done. Not yet. He didn't stop his movements and this time, one climax immediately led her into another and Odysseus thought she might collapse from the immense pleasure.

"Please," she pleaded, "don't stop."

He didn't. He began to touch himself, unable to keep from his own desire. The more he pleasured her, the more she writhed beneath him, the closer he came to his own release. It was sheer ecstasy, the two of them together in the hallway, loving each other the way humans were intended to love. He wouldn't let himself climax until he knew that she couldn't take any more of his touch.

But then she surprised him. She pulled away, brought him up from his knees, turned around so that she was facing the wall, and brought his hand around and down between her legs.

"Go back inside me and tease me," she said.

He pulled her hips back, allowing him to slide inside of her, his hard cock throbbing and begging for her body. And then he gently used his fingers the same way he had used his tongue. His thrusts were gentle at first, but then he became absolutely wild with desire and began to thrust heavily. He had lost count of how many times she had climaxed. His own release had been building for some time, but he wasn't sure he was ready for this beautiful, passionate moment to end.

"I'm close," he whispered in her ear.

"Me too," she said.

He didn't stop the movement of his hips or of his fingers and before he knew it, they were climaxing together, their bodies crescendoing into pure bliss. He pulled away and nearly collapsed to the ground in a heap, but managed to keep himself upright. He met his wife's gaze and she smiled brightly, seemingly just as dizzy as him. They stood there for a moment, collecting themselves, before deciding to go back to the stadium to watch the rest of the tourney. And as they did, Odysseus couldn't help but think that he was the luckiest man alive and how close he had come to ruining it.

Chapter Thirty

Slow and Steady

The Spider's Web,
Vathi, Ithaca
Greece

"I understand you are an engaged man now," the woman said, pouring herself a glass of brandy.

Antinous shrugged. "Makes no difference," he said, unbuttoning his vest. "My money is the same as it was before, is it not?"

The woman chuckled. "Never imagined you as the marrying type," she said, pouring him a glass of brandy, too. "I was just surprised to hear the news, is all."

He sighed. "I do not pay you to talk to me about gossip."

"You haven't paid me at all yet. I believe your tab is quite high at this point."

He reached into his pocket and produced a handful of coins and tossed them on the table. It was at least fifteen pounds, much more than he could possibly have owed this woman, he felt certain. "Does that suffice?"

She smiled, set her glass of brandy down and began to undo the bodice of her dress. In a moment the dress slipped off of her shoulders and fell to the floor, revealing a stunning and risqué undergarment made of red and black lace. Antinous was aroused immediately and motioned for her to go to the bed.

"The same routine as always?" she asked.

He shook his head. "No. I have something special planned tonight."

She raised her eyebrows. "Oh?"

"Lay on your back," he said, removing the rest of his clothes and walking towards the bed.

She did as instructed and Antinous carefully spread her legs wide, smiling down at her beautiful body. His eyes flitted up to meet hers.

"I'd like to put my mouth there," he said, running his fingers along the inside of her legs. "Do you consent?"

She smiled. "Would it matter if I did not?"

He furrowed his eyebrows. "Yes, Avalanna. It would matter a great deal."

She raised her eyebrows, her smile unwavering. "Would it truly?" She moaned. "That makes me want you all the more."

He grinned. "Do you consent?"

She nodded. "Yes, I do. Very much so."

His mouth was between her legs a moment later. He had never done this with Avalanna before, but he thoroughly enjoyed what it did to the other women he was with. Whore or not, the sounds they made, the ways they writhed and melted at his touch and begged for more, the ways it all made him feel like Zeus himself, kept him returning to this practice. He heard the ways these women spoke of their other customers, how little pleasure they got from them, how frequently they pretended to climax so that the customers wouldn't get angry. It disgusted him. Not the way they talked of it, but how commonplace it was for men to be so thoroughly boring. And why was it the woman's fault if the man couldn't bring her to climax? Was he the only member of his sex with an imagination?

Antinous reveled in the pleasure he gave to the women he paid. He intended to make himself renowned in every whore house in Ithaca. Well, as renowned as he could be without drawing attention to himself from the Duke of Ithaca. But, seeing as Odysseus was away from Ithaca just then and likely wouldn't return for weeks, Antinous had taken the liberty of enjoying himself this evening. It had been some time since he had last frequented The Spider's Web, and as he slid his tongue along Avalanna's flesh, he was glad he had decided to visit.

It wasn't just how he felt in these moments of physical intimacy. He wanted the women to enjoy their time with him, that much was true. And he did, indeed, enjoy giving them pleasure, hearing them shout his name. But it was also knowing how few of the other customers would do this with their whores that made him feel superior. It showed him that, despite what some may think about him, he was not an entirely worthless young man. There was, at least, one area wherein he thrived while others utterly failed.

Odysseus, he knew, was likely his only real competition in this arena. There was passion and desire between him and Penelope. If

Antinous would ever have the opportunity of stealing Penelope away from Odysseus, he had to compete with the duke as a lover. This, therefore, was practice. Fun, enjoyable, pleasurable practice, for every time he gave a woman this kind of experience, she gave him the same pleasure back tenfold.

Avalanna's moans filled him with raging passion. She sounded amazing, her groans and whimpers making him throb with desire. She wasn't pretending. Not with him. It took less than ten minutes for her to climax, and so he decided to stay where he was and tease her. It wasn't all about her, after all. He was here to have his own fun, and it was such fun to give them pleasure initially, make them want more of it, and then deny them. It was something he had stumbled on accidentally, and now was an experience he craved like wine.

He waited until he could tell she was close again before he stopped, pulled his tongue away and stared down at her bare flesh.

"What," she gasped, looking down at him. "No, why did you –"

She gasped as he let his tongue return and start again, only this time much more gently, as though he was hardly touching her. She writhed beneath him, clearly torn between pleasure and aching, her moans turning to the most beautiful whimpers of desperation.

"Do you like it?" he asked, pulling away again.

"Yes!" she exclaimed.

"Then, should I keep going?"

"Yes!" she said, even louder.

He did as she wanted, alternating between his usual, gentle touch swirling in circles around the sensitive peak, and then pulling away to where he could just barely feel her against him. Over and over he did this, bringing her as close to the edge as he could, and then stopping.

She didn't know it, but he was doing the same to himself, stroking his hardened cock every time he touched her and then stopping every time he pulled away. This was something else he had discovered by accident, and it was the most fun he had ever had with his own body.

Avalanna was nothing but moans and whimpers. She couldn't even ask him to keep going in full sentences. He smiled, genuinely happy that he could make a woman feel like this. How so many men could ignore this with their wives, he didn't know. But he didn't think he could ever live without this. Even when he married Abigail, he intended for this to be part of their bedding ritual. He may not have loved or cared about his intended, but he would have been lying if he said he was not greatly looking forward to bringing her this same pleasure. Some men were cruel in bed with their wives, and Antinous knew that would never be him. No, he would be gentle with her; he would bring her more pleasure than she could imagine, and she would worship him all the more for it. And that, too, would ultimately work in his favor.

He was too close to his own release thinking about that, and so he refocused his attention on Avalanna. It was time to end the teasing though because he wanted her fully now, needing her throbbing around his cock. He pressed his tongue against her, but his movements were agonizingly slow. He could feel her hardening against him and knew she was close.

"Oh god," she said, her breathing growing faster, deeper. "Oh god, Antinous, please..."

He couldn't help himself. He pulled away one last time and watched as the peak throbbed over and over, as if it too was begging him to come back, to keep going, to give the release.

"No!" she shouted and sounded as though she might cry. "No, please!"

He smiled and pressed a kiss to the inside of her thigh and then returned and let his tongue move across her again, still so wonderfully slow. But it was more than enough. The release built so slowly and Avalanna cried out in pleasure over and over, begging her body to just let it happen, until finally it did. She arched her back and screamed – truly screamed – with more pleasure than Antinous had ever seen her express.

Before the orgasm was done, though, he moved up above her and slid himself inside of her, his own body now desperate for climax. As he thrusted, she climaxed again, looking into his eyes with wonderment and, dare he say it, admiration. He really thought that she would do anything for him then, and that made him even harder. But he wasn't going to let himself climax that easily. He did to himself what he had done to her, brought himself to the edge only to stop and deny the release.

The longest he had been able to tease himself was twenty minutes. This time, he intended to go as long as possible. Over an hour later, he could barely thrust even once without threatening to climax. Avalanna could see how close he was and shoved him onto his back. She stared down at him and rocked her hips as slowly as she could, sliding herself up and down along him. He lifted one hand to cup one of her breasts.

"How long do you want me to drag this out?" she asked.

He grinned. "Make me beg."

She smiled and something akin to wickedness flashed in her eyes. Everything after that was a blur of flesh and blissful agony. All he knew was that he had never known so much pleasure in his life as when she was in control and did to him what he had done to her. Only she took it further, brought him even closer to the edge before stopping, and it created within him a feeling of climax without the full release. He wanted more of that. And she gave it to him until he couldn't take it anymore.

"Please," he begged, "oh god, please, let me!"

She smiled down at him. "No, I do not think I will."

He blinked as she sat there, straddled atop him, unmoving. He breathed heavily, his release on the edge. He both wanted it to fall over that edge, and reveled in her refusal to let him climax. And the way she looked down at him, the wicked lust and pleasure in her eyes, made him believe that if he was ever going to be in love, it would be with this woman, right here, right now.

She smiled and slid her hands down her abdomen, down in between her legs and began to fondle herself. It was slow play meant to torture him even more, and how he loved it. He let the desire and the lust wash over him time and time again, his body aching, yearning, pleading for some kind of touch. If she would just move her hips a little, he would climax.

"Please," he said when the yearning became too intense. "Please let me."

She shook her head. "No. Not until I've had another."

But she was moving her fingers so slowly, it would take forever for her to climax again. He was still so close, so ready for the release.

"Avalanna, I'm begging you, please," he said, genuinely feeling that he would go mad if she didn't let him climax soon.

She giggled. "You really want it, don't you?"

He nodded. "I need it, please!"

She still did not move. But he could feel her tightening around him.

"Beg more," she said, her fingers still sliding back and forth across herself.

"I don't..." he let out a breathless laugh as she continued to slowly tighten around him. It wasn't enough to make him climax, but it did inch him ever so much closer. "I won't last, Avalanna, please, please."

"Yes," she moaned. "More, Viscount Capshaw. Beg more."

"I will do anything," he said, and he meant it. He meant every word. "I will say anything, just please move even a little! Please! I need you!"

Gods, she felt glorious. Her muscles clenched around him as another climax washed over her and she slowly rocked her hips. The movements were agonizingly, blissfully slow and sent him into a tailspin of ecstasy. He didn't think the release itself would ever break over him; it just kept building and building and then her hips stopped moving. She was still touching herself. She was even still climaxing, or perhaps was having another climax altogether, but she stopped moving just as he neared the edge of his own release and for a moment, he thought she had ruined it.

But then it crashed over him.

Hard.

He screamed, quite literally, as the biggest release he had ever had in his life fell over his entire body. The release was unlike anything he had ever experienced. It was as though every release she had denied him had combined together and fell over him all at once, until his entire body was spent.

They lay next to each other, breathing heavily.

"I envy your fiancé," Avalanna said.

Antinous smiled but didn't respond. Yes, he was looking forward to all of this with Abigail, too. She was so innocent, so unassuming, that he was certain she would go from loving him on their wedding day to worshiping him after their wedding night. And that he only wanted so Penelope would see what she was missing. The more Abigail praised him, the more she talked about how happy she was in their marriage, the more Penelope would see what she could have had. And he was no fool – he knew that Penelope wouldn't be jealous at first. She was still happy with Odysseus, but that would change. And he would be the ideal husband until he had his chance with Penelope. What he did after that, he didn't know.

He would figure all of that out later.

Key List of Characters and Who They Really Are:

Not all of these characters are in this book, but they are the Olympians I have chosen to utilize in this series.

Baron Zachary Thunderstone: Zeus
Baroness Harriet Calf: Hera
Ms. Allyson Raport:Athena
Ms. Arabella Stag:Artemis
Baron Patterson Fish:Poseidon
Mr. Algernon Wolf:Ares
Dame Astoria Rose:Aphrodite
Baron Harper Cypress:Hades
Mr. Archibald Lyre:Apollo

Dame Daniella Torch:Demeter

Sir Hawthorn Satchel:Hermes

Sir Hendricks Gavel:Hephaestus

Dame Helaine Sconce:Hestia

Mr. Emerson Arrow:Eros